Poison Pen

by

Rose Boone

Credits:

Author Photo: Mary DuPrie Studios

Prologue

We all want the American Dream: good marriage, good job, a house with a picket fence, and 2.5 kids. Well, I had all of that. Kevin, my husband, was handsome, personable, and a hard worker. I've been employed at my job at General Motors for 20 years. My kids: Kevin Jr. (KJ) and Myra, are the kind of low-maintenance kids every parent prays for. We even bought our first house...and it actually had a white picket fence.

That's when things changed. My suburban dream quickly became a seemingly never-ending nightmare that I couldn't wake up from. My marriage fell apart and I was downsized out of a job. But that wasn't the worst of it. I started being stalked by a crazy person...a woman whom I thought was my friend.

Now, I want you to grab something to drink and a cozy place to read because the story I'm about to tell you is going to blow your mind...

Chapter One
1986

Scrambled eggs, bacon, toast, a bowl of fruit, and a cup of milk. That was the breakfast I served KJ and Myra at seven o'clock every morning before I drove them to school. It was nutritious, easy to prepare, stuck to their ribs—and they hated it. At the tender ages of seven and eight years old, my kids acted like eating breakfast would be the death of them. KJ routinely often hid the eggs under his slice of toast and Myra fed her portion of bacon to our dog, Sheba. Neither of them realized I was aware of their clandestine activities. I'm their mother, I know everything. I didn't expect them to eat everything, but if they downed enough to keep them full for the five hours before they'd eat lunch at school, I was happy.

"Hey, baby," Kevin said, adjusting his necktie as he plopped down in the chair. "Hey kids."

"Hey, Daddy!" KJ and Myra said in chorus.

Kevin gripped the handle of his favorite coffee mug and spoke to the kids while he scanned the front page of the newspaper.

"KJ," take that toast off those eggs and eat 'em. Baby girl...stop feeding Sheba your bacon."

"How did you see that?" Myra asked in the singsong voice she used whenever she spoke to her dad.

Kevin peered up from his newspaper long enough to wink at her and say, "Because I'm your daddy. I see everything."

"Y'all hurry up and eat," I said. "We've got to leave in ten minutes." I directed my attention to Kevin. "Babe, do you want something else before I sit down?"

"No thanks. I'm gon' chomp on this bacon and toast. I need to hurry up and get going too."

"Don't eat too much of that bacon. You know your pressure will spike on you without warning."

Kevin sipped on his coffee and gave me the "thumbs up" with his free hand.

"Why are you wearing your jogging suit?" Myra asked.

"Myra, I told you that I work from home now."

"How do you feel about that?" Kevin asked. "It's only been a couple of weeks, so I don't have much of an opinion at this point."

"I get that, but you worked at GM for a decade. You had a routine. I know it probably feels awkward doing something different."

"It did at first, but I'm kind of getting used to being a stay-home mommy."

"I can't lie, I'm getting used to hot cooked meals every day when I get home. This is a new routine that I could get used to."

"Speaking of routine, there is something I've been wanting to talk to you about." I looked over at KJ and Myra. They were both staring at me. "Why are y'all in grown folk business? KJ, grab the car keys off the counter and y'all go sit in the car. I'll be out there in a second."

Myra, being the daddy's girl that she is, sprang from her chair and ran around the table to give Kevin a hug and kiss. KJ, who detested public displays of affection (even inside our house was considered public to him if a third party could witness), gave Kevin a fist bump and headed to the door.

"I got the front seat!" Myra shouted.

"I get the front seat because I'm the oldest," KJ said.

"So, what's on your mind?"

"It's Caren."

"What about her?"

"Well, you know I've been side-eyeing her since they bought their house in the neighborhood."

"First of all, they're a few blocks over. You make it sound like they are on this block."

"She would've been on this block if she'd had her way. I'm glad they were able to buy a house, but I can't lie, I'm glad the financing fell through for the one they tried to buy on this block."

"Yeah, I've heard you say that a time or two...or three...or four."

"Whatever," I said and sipped my coffee.

"Babe, I've gotta get going. Whatever you need to say you have..." he looked at his wristwatch, "...four minutes to say it."

"Before I got laid off, you know I come up Willow Street."

"Un-hmm."

"Well, you know the way their house is positioned on Magnolia Street—two houses off the corner—she can see all of the cars that are crossing the intersection of Willow and Magnolia."

"And your point is?"

"My point is...every day when I used to come home from work, I passed that intersection. I turned our block and pulled into our driveway. Before I could get my stuff out of the car, my cellphone would ring—it was always Caren."

"I believe you've told me this before."

"I did tell you. I told you that at first I couldn't figure out how she always knew to call me right when I was getting home from work and then one day, I figured it out—"

"You said she must've been watching you from her kitchen window and timed you."

"Yes!"

"Babe, that's old news. You don't even work at GM anymore and don't keep the same hours, so let it go."

"I'd like to let it go, but she won't let me."

"What do you mean?"

"I mean it's started again. Ever since I lost my job and been home, she's been monitoring my comings and goings. And I know you're going to say I'm being paranoid—"

"You know me well."

"Yes, I do. So, last week I took a different route home. I drove up Lilly Street and then turned onto our block from the other end. She had no way to see me come home."

"So, it worked. You were able to avoid her."

"Yes, it worked. But more importantly, it got her to expose herself."

"How so?"

"She called me yesterday and asked me what route I used to come home."

Kevin arched an eyebrow.

"Un-huh, you gotta admit, that's weird."

"She definitely told on herself by asking that question." Kevin glanced at his wristwatch. "Look babe, I'll admit…she's weird. But it's a harmless kind of weird. Now, if you come home one day and I find Sheba boiling in a pot like Glenn Close did that rabbit in that movie, Fatal Attraction, then you'll see me get riled up. Until then," he leaned over and kissed my forehead, "I don't think she is worth the space you are letting her occupy rent free in your pretty little head." Kevin grabbed another strip of bacon. "I'm out of here."

I savored my coffee. My thoughts of Caren and her spooky ways swirled around my head. I envisioned her hiding in the shrubs that align my front yard. Peering at me from behind the trees in my backyard. Once, I thought I saw her looking in my bedroom window. It ended up being the shadow from a tree. Kevin was right—I was letting Caren live rent free in my head.

"One more thing," Kevin said, snapping me out of my trance. "The kids are still arguing over the front seat out here. You might wanna come see about 'em."

Chapter Two

When I stepped outside into the garage, KJ and Myra were standing next to the front passenger door of my car. They both had a hold of the door handle and refused to let it go.

"I know one thing, if y'all break my door handle I'm gon' break your butts."

"I called for the front seat first, Mama," Myra whined.

"I'm the oldest and I automatically get the front seat in the morning."

"And what rule book is that written in?" I asked.

"Huh?"

"Un-huh, you can't answer because you made that crap up. Sit in the back and let your sister sit in the front seat."

KJ released the door handle with a huff and pinched Myra as he moved past and opened the back door.

"Ouch! Mama, he pinched me!"

I looked at KJ through my rearview mirror. "What have I told you about pinching her?"

KJ folded his arms and looked out the window.

"Since you wanna pinch on her and then disrespect me, I've got a little news for you. She's going to ride in the front seat for the rest of the week and you are going to clean up her room every Saturday for the rest of this month."

KJ folded his arms tighter.

"Do you wanna clean up her room for two months?"

"No."

"What?"

"No, ma'am."

"Then you'd better your fix your face."

The three-block ride to Tidwell Elementary School was a quiet one. Myra spent most of the ride rubbing the meaty part of her right arm which was still smarting from KJ's pinch. KJ did *fix* his face like I ordered, but he never looked at me. I hung a right and got in the block long line that snaked through the neighborhood adjacent to the school and onto the school campus. The cars in the long line inched forward a few feet and stopped. This stop and go movement lasted for nearly ten minutes. When we got to the front of the school, I noticed Myra's teacher, Miss Lindsay, was standing along the curb with a thermos in her hand. She greeted Myra when she exited my car and waved at me.

"Hey, Mrs. Sloan," she shouted. "She's such a good girl."

"Thanks!" I shouted.

I turned to say good-bye to KJ, but he'd slipped out of the car while I was exchanging pleasantries with Myra's teacher.

That damn boy is stubborn just like his daddy. That's okay, he'll need me before I need him. At some point he's gon' come whining to me about something. Mama always wins.

I didn't have time to worry about KJ and his attitude, I'd tell Kevin and let him deal with that situation later that night. I, on the other hand, had more important things to worry about like getting my morning three-mile walk in, buying groceries, and getting my car inspected.

I worked up a good lather at the park; stretching my usual three-mile walk an extra quarter mile. Afterwards, I went home to change out of sweaty clothes and hydrate. I had a craving for a strawberry and banana smoothie, so I grabbed the ingredients and my blender—which Kevin teased had more buttons that an airplane cockpit—and started to prepare a drink that would keep me feeling full until dinner that evening.

My blender can sound like a lawnmower once it gets going. Which is why I guess I didn't hear Caren enter my home.

"Uhh!" I screamed. My heart threatening to burst through my chest. "You scared the crap out of me!"

"I'm so sorry," Caren said. "I knocked on the front door and rang the bell. I could hear your blender in here and I know you can't hear anything when it's on. The door was unlocked so I just let myself in. I hope you don't mind."

"It's not that I have a problem with you coming in. You just startled me."

"I'm sorry." She pointed at my blender. "That thing needs an oil change. It's as loud as a tractor trailer."

You wouldn't know that if you hadn't just barged into my house without an invitation, I thought. *Nothing worse than a rude person who is oblivious to their rudeness.*

"Yeah, I guess so." I wiped the adrenaline induced perspiration dotting my forehead. "Umm, I'm making myself a smoothie before I leave out to run some errands. Do you want one?"

"You need me to babysit next week?"

"Excuse me."

Caren pointed at my wall-mounted wax board calendar stuck to my refrigerator. It's where I kept my daily itinerary. I used it in case my kids or Kevin came home looking for me. At a glance, they could see where I was and an approximate time when I'd return home.

"I see you have a doctor's appointment next week. I can babysit for you while you go to the doctor."

Really woman. Who reads someone else's calendar? Damn she's rude.

"Umm, no. I've already made arrangements. But thanks for asking." I poured my drink into a plastic cup. An awkward silence, that made the hairs on the back of my neck dance, waffled between us. "Like I said, I'm about to run some errands. Sooo…"

"Right, right, don't let me keep you. I'd ride with you, but I have some errands of my own to do."

How could you ride with me when I never invited you? This woman is a trip.

"Okay then," I said and walked toward the front door hoping she'd take the non-verbal cue and leave. "Maybe we can link up later this week."

"That'll work," Caren said as she stepped outside on my porch. "By the way, you still haven't told me what you want me to do while you're on vacation."

"Excuse me."

"Vacation. Remember you and Kevin asked me to check on your house while you guys leave for vacation in two weeks."

"Oh yeah, right. It's not much. I'll just need you to put the mail in the house and water the flowers in here. We're taking Sheba with us, so you won't have to deal with a pet."

Caren stuck out her hands and wiggled her fingers.

"What's wrong?" I asked.

"Uhh, if you want me to do those things, I'm going to need a key."

"Right, right…a spare key." I stepped away from the door and retrieved a spare key from the junk drawer in the kitchen. "Here you go."

Caren cupped her ear like she was waiting to hear something.

"What?" I asked.

"You never told me the alarm code. A sista don't wanna get arrested for breaking and entry."

"Oh, yeah, the alarm code." I unconsciously started to wring my hands and rock on the balls of my feet like a contestant on The Price is Right when they are trying to decide what price to quote on an item and everyone in the audience is shouting numbers at them. "4884."

"Forty-eight, eighty-four. That's easy to remember." Caren spun on her heels and walked away. She waved her hand over her shoulder without looking back. "Don't worry my friend, I'll treat your house like it's my own."

That's what I'm afraid of, I thought as I fought back the urge to run over to her and snatch my house key from her hand.

Chapter Three

We were excited to leave to go on vacation. We were going on a road trip to the beautiful state of Arizona to see the Grand Canyon—one of the top sites on my bucket list. I could hardly contain my excitement. The kids were staying at my sister's house across town for the seven days we'd be gone, and I'd been packed and ready to go for a week. Unfortunately, Kevin wasn't. He waited until the last minute to pack. And when I say last minute, I mean the night before. As a result, he walked into the living room on our day of departure looking like a zombie.

"Babe, it's almost six, we're already thirty minutes behind schedule," I said.

Kevin waved his hand lazily as if trying to swat away my words. He staggered into the kitchen.

"I just need a cup of coffee to wake up," he growled.

"That's why God made McDonalds. We can get coffee on the road. I've already put the suitcases in the car. I have the map ready. I'll drive for a few hours until you wake up." I shoved him toward the door. "C'mon, I waited too long for this trip. I'm not about to let you get us off track because you procrastinated."

As I pulled out of the driveway, I had a fleeting thought: *I hope this weird woman doesn't go snooping through our things while we're gone.*

Kevin went to sleep five minutes into the drive. I spent the time listening to soft music, enjoying the scenery, and getting lost in my thoughts. It wasn't until he yawned and made noise while stretching that I remembered he was next to me.

"I got your coffee," I said. "It should still be warm. I just bought it thirty minutes ago."

"Thanks, babe." Kevin sipped the brew. "Pretty good."

"Two creams and five sugars, just like you like it."

"That's my girl."

We drove in silence for nearly thirty minutes before Kevin spoke up.

"A penny for your thoughts."

I shrugged and said, "My mind is all over the place, but mostly, I keep thinking about Caren."

"I swear, I don't understand why you are even friends with her. It's clear that you don't really like her."

"It's not that I don't like her' she just acts kind of weird at times."

"Well, you learned that when she let her son ruin your groceries in the car and then got mad at you when you told him to stop."

"Yeah, I guess that could be considered a red flag, but the truth of the matter is, you have a lot of parents these days who don't like you saying anything to their bad ass kids."

"True." He sipped his coffee. "That was your opportunity to bail on the relationship."

"I did for a little while."

"A little while is not permanent." He paused to admire a billboard before continuing. "You even agreed to be the Godmother to her daughter."

"She pressured me into it. Besides, I sort of felt indebted to her because she helped me get the job at GM."

"I get it but being a child's Godparent is serious. You're making a vow to step in and be a surrogate parent in the event something happens to the parents. You just don't commit to something like that."

"That job helped us get out of that tiny apartment."

"I can't argue with that. That place was so small I could stand in the living room and touch the entrance to the kitchen, bedroom, and bathroom."

"That's my point. We needed that job in the worst way." I stopped talking long enough to move past an eighteen-wheeler. "I don't know...I just thought she'd be different. I mean, I don't remember her having such a fickle personality back in college."

"Yeah, but how well did you really know her in college?"

"It was a casual acquaintance. She was Felicia's friend. And since Felecia and I were roommates, it was only natural that I became cool with her friends. When we bumped into each other at the supermarket, I was excited to see a familiar face. You know we didn't know anyone in Detroit."

"Nobody."

"Right. When I saw her, I figured I'd at least have one person I can talk to. Besides, her and Robert had already been living here a year, so I relied on her to help me learn the area. Then when she gave me the job lead for General Motors, I thought she was a godsend."

"Satan was an angel."

"Hush, she ain't that bad...just a little weird at times."

"Well, it's a little too late to be paranoid about her. You entrusted her with a key to our house."

"I didn't have many options."

"You could have asked Debbie to check on the house."

"Debbie is already babysitting our kids for a week. I didn't think it was fair to ask her to check on the house too."

Kevin nodded. He placed his hand on top of my hand that was at the two o'clock position on the steering wheel.

"It's too late to change things now. We're gone and she's got the key. Anything of value is locked in the safe in the attic." He took a long gulp of his coffee and then pointed at a rest stop sign. "Get off at this rest stop exit so I can use the bathroom. We'll switch so you can get some rest while I drive...slow poke."

The Grand Canyon was as breathtaking as it is in photos and on television. I even suppressed my fear of heights and walked out on the furthest ledge, leaned against the railing, and let Kevin take a picture of me. It was hands down the best vacation we'd had as a couple. The conversations we had about our kids, aspirations, and plans for future vacations, were as precious and memorable to me as that massive hole in the earth that we drove all those miles to go see.

Unfortunately, all good things must come to an end. And thoughts of our fairytale vacation quickly vanished once we returned to our home.

Kevin and I were mentally spent by the time we pulled into our driveway and parked. It was nearly nine at night and we agreed that the task of toting the luggage into the house could wait until the next morning.

As we entered the house I was struck with an eerie feeling. I felt like someone was hiding inside. I now realize that it wasn't an actual person, but it was negative energy. Negative energy that had been left behind by the person I trusted to housesit for us in our absence.

While Kevin made a beeline for the bathroom, I headed straight to the nearest light switch. In fact, I turned on every light switch in the house. With my keys between my fingers like tiny daggers that would slice any fleshly being that leapt out from the shadows, I peeked behind every door and in every corner to make sure we were alone.

"Bae, what are you doing?" Kevin called out.

"Checking for intruders!"

"Woman, ain't nobody in here. Turn off all those lights!"

I ignored him. Checking the house for prowlers was his job. Instead, he decided to make his first stop the bathroom. So, as far as I was concerned, he put his bowels over my safety—his opinion at that point became irrelevant.

Because I had concerns about Caren snooping, I decided to pull a trick I used to do as a child to check if my siblings or parents had rummaged through my things. I purposely positioned a few items in the top drawer of my chest of drawers. A sock with blue stars on it was placed in such a way that only one star faced the opening of the drawer—two stars faced the opening when I looked inside. An envelope that contained an old electricity bill was positioned with the tip touching the star covered sock; that bill was on the other side of the drawer when I looked inside—she had been reading our bills?

Lastly, I left three strands of hair on a smooth white shirt positioned at the far-left corner of the drawer—the hairs were gone, and the shirt was crumpled.

"Baby!" I yelled.

"What!"

"Come here!"

"Why?"

"I think she went through my drawer!"

Kevin let out an audible sigh. Moments later, I could hear him yanking tissue off the role and then the toilet flushed. He exited the bathroom, paused to wash his hands, and then made his way over to where I stood.

"What are you in here being paranoid about?"

"I put some things in this drawer that would indicate if someone went into this drawer while we were gone. Everything I did has been changed."

"Maybe it's just a coincidence. Did you check some of the other drawers in here?"

"I don't need to. I was only concerned about this drawer because…"

The reality slapped me in the face like the wind that whipped around the Grand Canyon. I tossed the clothes aside in the top drawer and shoved my hand all the way to the back where I kept a little purple Crown Royal drawstring pouch. The pouch was there, but the contents weren't.

"…she took one of the joints."

"What?"

"There were three joints in this drawer. Now there are only two."

"Are you sure you didn't smoke it?"

"I'm positive."

"Do you think you might have told her about where you kept your stash when you were high."

I looked at Kevin with the same glare Judge Judy does when a defendant gets on her nerves. He held up his hands and backed up.

"Okay…bad joke. Sorry. But babe, you can't really be that mad."

"Why can't I?"

"Because you know she's a snoop. You remember the first time she came over to our tiny apartment and asked to use the bathroom? You told me you heard the shower curtain pull back; she was checking to see if the tub was clean."

I nodded.

"Okay then. If a person is crazy on Monday, she gon' be crazy on Friday. You knew what she was capable of, yet you still chose to trust her." He chuckled. "This is kind of a self-inflicted wound."

"This ain't no laughing matter, Kevin. I told you I was concerned she might go through our stuff, and she did. I should've followed my gut." I sat on the bed and buried my face in my hands. "Ain't no tellin' what else she snooped through. I feel violated."

Kevin sat next to me on the bed and placed a comforting hand in the small of my back.

"It is a violation, babe. Do you want to confront her, or do you want me to do it?"

"I'll do it. I'm the one who gave her the key. This is a woman-to-woman conversation we need to have face-to-face. I'm too tired to deal with it now. I'll confront her tomorrow."

Chapter Four

I was more physically exhausted than I realized after our vacation. I slept until noon the next day. Fortunately, my sister and I agreed before we left town that she's bringing Myra and KJ to school on Monday and I'd pick them up.

Kevin, a consummate work-a-holic was ready to get back to his office an hour after we left the Grand Canyon. So, I was not surprised to see a message on the wax board in the kitchen from him saying he'd gone into the office.

I was happy to see that Kevin brought our luggage in the house at some point before he left. We bought so much memorabilia and extra clothes that we needed to go to Walmart and buy an additional suitcase.

After I took a cold shower to help me wake up, I brewed a fresh pot of coffee and commenced to washing all the clothes that we brought with us on the trip. By two-thirty I'd washed everything I could find, watched a few of my favorite daytime shows, and was preparing to go and pick my kids up from school. Since I knew Caren was a volunteer teacher, I figured I'd see her standing outside doing afterschool pickup duty with several other teachers. I intended to park my car, pull her to the side—away from any witnesses, give her a piece of my mind, and get my housekey back—but none of that happened.

"Hey, Mama!" Myra squealed as she climbed in the car and gave me a kiss and hug. "I've missed you."

"I missed you too, Baby. Where is your brother?"

"Over there playing with those boys."

I spotted KJ horseplaying a few yards away, so I honked to get his attention. He gathered up his things and scurried to the car.

"Hey, Mama!"

"Hey, Baby. I would hug you, but you're all sweaty. And you smell like outside."

"That's because I've been outside playing."

"Stop being flip and buckle your seatbelt." I scanned the area but didn't see Caren. "Have y'all seen Mrs. Caren today?"

"No!" the kids said in unison.

I stopped my search and pulled out of the parking lot.

"Mama, can I walk to school with Jeffrey, Patrick, and DeMarcus. They walk to school every day and asked me if I could come with them. Pleeeease!"

"Let me think about. I'll give you an answer after I talk to your dad."

KJ sat at the kitchen table doing his math homework while Myra sat on the living room floor and watched cartoons while I cooked. This was the part of being a stay-at-home wife that I loved the most. For years, I worked twelve-hour shift at GM. By the time I made it home from work I was often too tired to think let alone cook. After taking the early buyout, I was able to drop my kids off at school, pick them up, and help them with their homework.

The phone startled me when it started ringing. I placed the spoon I used to stir the spaghetti I slaved over on the counter and answered.

"Hello."

"Hey, Beauty, this is Pete from across the street."

"Oh, hey, Pete. What's up?"

"I just called to let you know that KJ is welcomed to walk to school with Jeffrey and his little buddy DeMarcus from up the block. You know I work over at the school in the Maintenance Department. I let 'em walk to school together—you know, it makes 'em feel like big boys—and then I bring them all home after school. Trust me, I drop them all off in front of their houses, and I don't leave until a parent comes to the door or they are inside safe."

I looked over at KJ, but he was too busy staring at the numbers in his workbook and counting on his fingers to notice me.

"Yeah, I guess it'll be okay to let him walk to school in the morning with the other boys."
Suddenly, the kid who was too into his studies to notice me, leapt from his chair and double-timed over to me. His little arms wrapped around my waist like an anaconda. He nearly squeezed the life out of me.

"But he has to wait to ride home with you—Mr. Pete—every day."

KJ nodded frantically.

"Alright, Pete. KJ will be out tomorrow morning at 7:30 in front of our house waiting for his little friends."

When I hung up the phone, I stared into KJ's eyes and said, "You miss that ride with Mr. Pete one time, and you'll never walk to school with your friends again. You understand me?"

"Yes! Yes! Yes!"

My son was on cloud nine. I was happy to be able to make him smile. Little did I know that decision would be the segue to an avalanche of drama.

Chapter Five

I pondered my decision long after that phone call ended. A part of me felt like I was shirking my parental duties. After all, I wasn't working. I should be the one dropping off and picking up my kids from school. Isn't that what conscience stay at home mothers do? Isn't that one of the unwritten rules in the "Homemaker" handbook?

By nightfall, my head was cluttered with more worst-case scenarios. The one that stuck to my mind like wallpaper was whether I was introducing my child to the possibility of being molested in some way. The news is saturated with accounts of coaches, priests, and boy scout troop leaders—men charged with teaching and protecting young boys—who sexually molest the boys they are sworn to look after. Pete seemed like a nice guy, but how well do you really know anyone? What if his easy to talk to and helpful ways were just a façade? Of course, I'd never heard of, or seen, him doing anything inappropriate to a child. In fact, his neighborhood reputation was above reproach. Still, KJ was my child and anything that happened to him after I gave my blessing would be partially my fault.

"You're doing what you always do," Kevin said as he climbed into bed.

"What's that supposed to mean? What are you trying to say?"

"Beauty, you have a bad habit of overthinking things. Not everything is a conspiracy. Everyone you meet doesn't have a hidden agenda. There are nice people in this world—people who want to help. I think Pete is one of those types of people. I've never heard anyone question his integrity. If I had, I would've already shut this down. But I haven't, so I'm not."

"I hear you, but—"

"But nothing, baby." Kevin propped up on both elbows and looked at me. "Look, you're a woman, so you don't get it. Boys are wired different. If you don't let him roll with his little friends, you'll be emasculating him and setting him up for some stressful days."

"Because I want to protect him? That's my job."

"And it's my job to keep him from being the kid that gets picked on at the playground. If you keep him from walking to school, you might as well write "bully me" on a sheet of paper and tape it to his backpack." Kevin leaned over and kissed my forehead. "Trust me on this one, he'll be fine walking to school with his friends and riding home with Pete."

The next day I was up at the crack of dawn. I read my bible, did some aerobics, and sipped on some coffee while I prepared the kids lunch bags. Kevin motored past like his hair was on fire.

"Love you, babe!" he tossed over his shoulder on his way out the door.

I doubt if he heard my response because the door slammed behind him before I could get it out. That was becoming more commonplace than I cared to admit. Kevin and I living our lives like it were a run-on sentence with no commas, semi-colons, or periods. At times, we seemed to have a drive-by marriage—tossing morsels of affection at each other the way people sit on park benches tossing pieces of bread to waddling pigeons.

"Mama, can I walk to school today?" Myra asked in her trademark whiny voice.

"No, honey. I'm bringing you to school."

"But KJ said he's walkin' to school today."

I could see KJ approaching from behind my tattle-tale daughter looking as proud as George Jefferson when he and Weezy bought their deluxe apartment on the east side. His smile was as wide as his face and his chest stuck out as if he wanted to have a ribbon pinned on his shirt.

"KJ, are you teasing your sister?"

"Nope." He grabbed the Pop Tart and his lunch bag. "I'm going now. Bye."

"Wait!"

"What, mama? They're gonna leave me!"

"No, they won't. Come here."

KJ pouted over to me and stayed still while I wet the tip of my thumb and got the remaining sleep couched in the corners of his eyes.

"I hope you brushed your teeth better than you washed your face." I dabbed away any moisture I created. "There you go…now you're ready. Now remember what we went over."

"I know, I know…make sure I am where Mr. Pete tells us to be after school. Make sure I say thank you. And always make sure I'm with one of my friends and don't be alone in the car."

I nodded to show approval and then sent him on his way with a flick of my wrist. I wanted so desperately to grab him and beg him not to leave me. But I knew I couldn't. I also knew that he'd shed me like a running back shedding a linebacker.

KJ met the other boys on the sidewalk in front of Jeffrey's house. The threesome gave each other dap like they were teenagers.

He's growing up so fast, I thought and choked back the desire to weep.

I watched them until their little bodies became mere blurs at the end of the block and vanished. If it weren't for the wall-mounted telephone's loud ring, those tears welling in my eyes would've spilled.

"Uh-um…hello."

"Hey, girl!"

"Oh, hey Caren."

"Are you okay?"

"Yeah, I'm fine. Just my allergies."

"Girrrl, don't I know. My allergies have been acting up on me too. What are you taking for them? Lately, I've been taking—"

"Caren, umm, I don't mean to cut you off, but I'm trying to get Myra ready for school."

"Oh, okay. I didn't call to keep you. I just called because I was looking out my window and I could have sworn I saw KJ walking down the street with some little boys."

"That was him. He begged me to start letting him walk to school with his little friends. I didn't want to, but Kevin didn't see a problem with it."

"He's probably right. It was three or four of 'em in a group, so they'll be safe. You can kiss him and love on him when you pick him up after school."

"I'm not picking him up."

"What?"

"Umm, Pete, my neighbor from across the street, is going to pick them up. His son Jeffrey was one of the little boys KJ was walking with. Pete works in Maintenance at the school. He's going to round them all up and bring them home."

My explanation was met with a silence that I found a tad bit odd at the moment, but in hindsight, I realize that it was extremely telling. Caren didn't approve of my new child transportation arrangement, but she knew better than to openly question me. My first inclination was to encourage her to speak up. I'm ashamed to admit it, but I was a little curious to hear her protest. Sort of like sneaking a peek at an accident scene on the highway as you slowly drive past; you know you shouldn't gawk, but you do. Fortunately, my inner voice trumped my curiosity on that day. A little voice in my head spoke to me before I could part my lips:

You don't owe her an explanation. Who cares what she thinks? Hurry up and get off the phone before she asks more ignorant questions that are none of her business.

"Well, I really have to get going. So, I'll call you later."

"That's fine. Talk to you later."

I was stretched out on my sofa struggling to keep my eyes from slamming shut while I watched a soap opera when my doorbell chimed. I peeled myself off the sofa and staggered to the front door. When I opened the door, I realized that Caren's definition of "later" was different than mine.

"Hey, girl!"

"Oh, hey."

"You look like you were sleeping."

"I was dozing off while watching television." There was that awkward silence again. It swirled between us like a subtle summer breeze.

"I didn't know you were coming."

"Yeah, I started to call you, but I wasn't doing anything, so I decided to walk over here. I needed the exercise anyway."

"Oh, okay. Umm, come on in."

"Girl, I really like the way you've decorated the place. I noticed that when I was housesitting for you."

"Thanks. Do you want something to drink?"

"I could use a bottle of water."

Caren followed me into the kitchen. I retrieved a bottle of water from the refrigerator and gave it to her.

"Thanks. I'm thirsty enough to drink this entire bottle in one gulp." She ripped the top off, took a swig, and pointed at the calendar on my refrigerator. "You need me to babysit."

"Huh?"

"I see you have a doctor's appointment next week. I can watch the kids for you."

"Uhh, no. Kevin will be home to watch them."

The fact that she was examining my calendar annoyed me. It annoyed me so much that the thought of her rummaging through my personal belongings came to my mind.

"You know, since I have you here, there is something I need to ask you."

"What's up?"

"Did you go through my drawers while I was out of town?"

I asked the question while she was in the middle of taking a drink. She froze with the bottle pressed against her lips. Her eyes widened and she looked like she wanted to somehow crawl inside that water bottle and disappear.

"Oh, umm, yeah. You know me, I'm a neat freak. While I was checking your house just to make sure everything was okay, I thought I heard something in your bedroom."

"Why would you think that?"

"I said I thought I heard something. I realized once I went in the room that it was your air conditioning unit turning on. It's right outside your bedroom window, right?"

I nodded. "But that doesn't explain you in my drawer."

"Yeah...about that. I saw a pair of socks on the floor. I picked them up and tossed them in the drawer. I'm sorry girl, I can't help being a neat freak." She held up her hands. "I didn't look inside the drawer. I just shoved the socks inside drawer and closed it." Caren glanced at her watch. "Girl, let me get back home. I need to start dinner before the kids get out of school."

Caren scurried toward the front door. She moved faster to leave than she did to come in.

"Guess who I spoke to yesterday!"

"Who?"

"Jessica Smith. You remember her from college?"

"Yeah. I didn't know y'all kept in touch."

"We talk every other month. I told her that you and Kevin went on vacation, and she was surprised to hear that."

"Why would she be surprised?"

"I think it's because she and I spoke around the time Kevin went to California to his family reunion and you went to New York for your family reunion. When she heard y'all went to separate reunions she said y'all marriage was on the rocks and wouldn't last. Girl, she was speechless when she learned y'all went to the Grand Canyon. She had to eat those words."

I opened the door and held it open for her to leave. The fact that she was talking about me to a woman we went to college with—a woman whom I barely remembered--irked me so much that I could feel a headache coming on. While rubbing my forehead I let my true feelings be known.

"I don't give a damn about Jessica's opinion. Tell her I said to worry about her own marriage."

"I know that's right," Caren said and stepped outside. Without looking back at me she said, "I'll talk to you later!"

As I watched her walk away, I rolled my eyes and thought: *You gon' be talking to yourself because I ain't answering the phone and if you come here again unannounced, I'm damn sure not opening the door.*

"Calm down," Kevin said. "You gon' let that woman give you an ulcer."

"I'm trying to calm down, but every time I turn around, she is doing something to annoy me. First she rummages through my drawer."

"Wait, wait...you admitted to me that you were rushing when we were packing and that some socks might have fallen on the floor."

"Yes."

"Well, you must admit that her excuse may be legitimate. And I've even mentioned to you that I wish that air conditioning unit was located somewhere else instead outside of our bedroom window."

41

"Well, what about her mentioning KJ walking to school?"

"She just mentioned she saw him. What's wrong with that?"

"Nothing, I guess. But there is definitely something wrong with her looking at my calendar."

"Babe, you got the damn calendar plastered on the refrigerator for the world to see. Stevie Wonder could see that you had a doctor's appointment."

"You're always defending her. What you got to say about her gossiping about our marriage?"

"That was messy of her, and it sounds like you called her on that. But let's keep it real...we gossip about other couples too. The bottom line is that Caren was supposed to keep that little conversation to herself."

"Yeah, she should have."

"What are you saying? Do you want to end your friendship with her?"

"Is what we have called a friendship?"

"You gave her the keys to her house, so I would hope you consider her a friend." Kevin sighed. "Look...I think you should just take a break from her. Maybe what y'all need is a little space."

"Yeah, maybe you're right."

"I know I'm right. Now, I've gotta get back to work. Did you cook?"

"Yeah. I cooked corn beef cabbage and cornbread."

"Are you inviting Caren over?"
Kevin laughed at his own joke, but I didn't.
"Too soon?" he asked.
"Much too soon," I said and hung up.

Chapter Six

An awkward silence hung over the dinner table that evening. The kids fiddled with their food. My thoughts were still on Caren and her weirdo ways. And I guess the best way to describe Kevin's behavior that evening was, aloof. It reminded me of that old song, *The Other Side of Town*, by The O'Jays. His body was there with me, but his eyes seemed to wander, and his thoughts drifted off into space.

"Y'all kids go on and put your plates on the counter," I said. "You're just playing with your food anyway."

The kids moved at breakneck speed. Nearly knocking each other over to get away from the table so they could go watch cartoons and play video games.

"Is there something wrong?" I asked.

Kevin sighed and stabbed a mound of cabbage with his fork. "Work. A lot to do and not much time to do it." He sipped his soda and cocked his head while looking at me. "You're asking me if I'm okay, when I should be asking you if you're okay."

"I'm fine," I said and shoved some food into my mouth. After I finished chewing and washed the food down, I said, "No, I'm not. I'm not fine and I'm tired of pretending I am."

"What's wrong?"

"It's Caren."

"You and that damn woman." Kevin shook his head pitifully. "I told you earlier…she's gon' give you an ulcer."

"Babe, I heard what you said earlier, and I hear what you are saying now, but I can't help it, she really gets on my nerves sometimes. I can't quite put my finger on it. It's like we're friends, but we're not. Have you ever had someone in your life who you can't really pinpoint their purpose or what value they bring to your world, but they remain in your life?"

Kevin thought for a minute.

"I guess the closest I ever experienced to that would be Harold Franklin. You remember Harold, tall, heavyset dude that I told you grew up on the same block with me."

"I do remember him," I said. "Didn't he die?"

"Yeah, he was killed in a drive-by. Ironically, the guy who killed him was someone he had a fight with while he was in prison."

"I don't remember that part."

"Yeah, Harold was locked up for three years after high school for selling drugs. By the time he came home from prison, a lot of his old friends were either dead, locked up, joined the military, or gone off to college. He was roaming the streets like a lost puppy."

"Bless his heart."

"Yeah, I felt sorry for him and told him to come over one day and just kick it. That was my first mistake. Before I knew it, he was at my house every day—all damn day. He started following me around like a stray cat after you feed it. He'd show up at my house ten in the morning during the summer and just hang around. All he wanted to do was tell jailhouse stories. At first, they were fun to listen to, but after a while, they got boring. He wasn't really bringing any value to my world."

"That's how I feel about Caren. She doesn't really bring any value to my world. Whenever she's around me, I feel an energy shift. It's like my spirits get low. All she wants to do is gossip." I paused to sip my soda. "Did I ever tell you about the time she prank called her friend?"

Kevin shook his head.

"This happened back when we first reconnected here. One day, she told me her gossip buddy, Susan—the one she gossiped too about me—contracted herpes from a guy she was sleeping with. Susan was very distraught and confided in Caren because she was looking for support and compassion."

"Let me stop you. If you know this was that woman's secrets, why did you sit there and listen to Caren be a blabber mouth?"

"I did tell her that she was wrong for talking about the lady, but she just kept spilling the woman's business. She told me that she disguised her voice like a man and called Susan in the wee hours of the morning...something like 4:00 a.m."

"And said what?"

"She just said: herpes...in a deep, slow, voice. And then she hung up."

"That's sick."

"Very. I felt so bad for Susan."

"Did you tell Caren that was a foul thing to do?"

"Of course, I did. I told her she was being mean and hurtful for no reason. She just chuckled and said, Susan would never know who it was that called. Then she tried to justify what she did by saying Susan wasn't sleeping well anyway, so it wasn't like she woke her up."

Kevin shook his head in disgust.

"I told her that wasn't the point. You are causing mental pain and suffering on someone that is supposed to be your friend. She turned to you in confidence."

"What did Caren say when you told her that?"

"She just laughed."

"Honestly, there's something sadistic about that. You know they say, hurt people...hurt people. Makes you wonder what kind of pain she's harboring to make her get a kick out of doing that to someone she calls a friend."

"I don't know what happened to her to make her that way, but whatever she went through it affected her brain because she's sick. A few weeks after she told me that story, she told me about a time when she had an incident at work. During one of her breaks, she went into the vending machine café to purchase a cup of coffee. She said, when it was her turn to use the machine, a racist white man cut in front of her. She didn't even bother arguing with him. She just went back to work and wrote him a threating letter."

"What did she say in the letter?"

"She wrote that some black men would catch him in the parking lot one day on his way to his car. Then she put the letter in the inner-departmental mail. I tried to correct her behavior again."

"Why?"

"What do you mean, *why*?"

"Why would you try to correct her for doing that? As far as I'm concerned, he had that coming. He bullied a woman. And a black woman at that." Kevin shook his head. "I agree that she might be a little off," he twirled his finger next to his ear to stress she might be coocoo, but I honestly don't have a problem with that one."

"Well, I told her she could get in trouble for sending that threatening letter, and maybe even lose her job. She should have said something to him face to face when he did it or tell a supervisor."

"I disagree. If he was bold enough to disrespect her then he was probably bold enough to attack her if she stood up to him." Kevin shrugged. "I'm sorry…I don't have a problem with that approach. His ass needed to be threatened."

"Well, my little advice didn't matter anyway because she didn't see anything wrong with her approach even when I mentioned she could have lost her job. She called him a racist fool who needed to be scared every day after work."

"I agree."

"Well, I'm convinced that her bizarre behavior is proof that she has some kind of personality and character disorder, and I just don't want to be around her. My grandma used to always say: 'A dog that'll bring a bone, will take a bone'. I know that every time she gossips to me about someone, she's running to other people and gossiping to them about me."

Kevin pointed his fork at me. "Now that point, I can't argue." He finished off his drink, leaned back, and patted his belly. "That was good, bae." He took his plate over to the kitchen sink and talked while he washed it off. "Let me be clear, I'm not saying Caren isn't weird—there is no denying that she is. All I'm saying is, she seems to really like you and want to be your friend. I think there are ways to manage the friendship without completely cutting her off. You just need to feed her with a long-handle spoon."

"I've tried to do that. But she keeps trying to get closer to me."

Kevin walked up behind me, leaned over, and kissed my forehead. "Then I suggest you make the spoon longer." He playfully pinched my cheek. "Now, I'm going take a shower." He paused and looked back at me. "You know, we had a motivational speaker come to our office last year. He was hired to come and try and boost morale. He talked about being a positive influence on people with negative attitudes. He was trying to drive home the point that we all have the power to make the energy in the workplace so positive that negativity can't co-exist. Weren't you talking about having a card game with some of your old co-workers?"

"Yes. We're actually supposed to do that this Saturday."

"Maybe you should invite her."

"Oh, no. I don't even want her around my other friends. She might infect them."

"Or," he held up a finger, "their positive energy might infect her."

Kevin turned on his heels and walked out of the dining room area before I could respond. I pondered his suggestion for a long time. As a matter of fact, I was still sitting at the dinner table thinking about it by the time he finished taking his shower.

"Damn, you're still sitting there?"

"I've just been thinking about what you said."

"Well, what are you going to do?"

I dropped my fork on my plate, sighed, and leaned back in my chair. After crossing my arms and wondering if I was crazy myself, I looked at him and said, "It's against my better judgment, but I'm going to invite her to come over and play cards with us."

Saturday seemed to come faster after Kevin talked me into inviting Caren. It was like the universe was anxious to watch a train wreck. I visualized God sitting around eating popcorn and chuckling at the travesty that He knew was about to take place.

I allowed Myra to attend a sleepover at her friend's house. KJ lobbied—successfully—to spend the night across the street at Jeffrey's house. Kevin went to hang out at a sports bar with some of his friends. I had the house all to myself.

I invited my old friends: Barbara, Lavern, and yes, Caren, but only Lavern and Caren were coming. Barbara called a few hours before we were scheduled to meet to let me know she couldn't make it because her grandmother died, and she was leaving town immediately. That killed the plans to play Spades. I had every intention of teaming Barbara up with Caren. Gin Rummy would have to be the game for the evening.

I rushed to a nearby supermarket and picked up some last-minute refreshments. I also grabbed a bottle of wine and a greeting card to send to Barbara. The moment I got back home, I made some deviled eggs and checked on some Swedish meatballs that were warming in my crock pot. Everything was going according to plans.

I told the ladies to be at my house at eight o'clock. You wanna guess who showed up thirty minutes early? Yep…Caren.

I'd just gotten out of the shower and was walking around wearing a bathrobe when the doorbell rang. I thought it was KJ coming back to grab a video game or some toy that he might have left before he went over to Jeffrey's house. But when I opened the door, "Ms. Negative" was standing there with a grin as wide as her face.

"Oh, hey…you're early."

"Yeah, I know," Caren said and barged in, "but I was eager to get out of that house. I needed a break from those kids. I ordered two large pizzas from Dominos so that they could have something to eat, and then I gave my husband the deuces and told him not to wait up for me."

"Oh…okay. Well, as you can see, I'm still not dressed. Make yourself comfortable while I go put on some clothes. There are some deviled eggs in the refrigerator and meatballs in the crockpot."

"Girl, I can smell 'em. I hope you don't mind if I dig in. I'm starving."

"Be my guest," I said and waved my hand at the crockpot.

I left her standing there peeking inside the crock pot. When I returned fifteen minutes later, she was sitting on one of the barstools with her elbows on the kitchen countertop. Her head was aimed downward, so I thought she'd dozed off.

"Caren."

Caren flinched like a child caught watching pornography.

"Oh, hey! I didn't hear you come back in here."

I craned my neck to see what she was looking at on the counter. She was looking at the card that I'd bought to give to Barbara.

"I was just reading this card," she said when she saw me staring at the card. "Did someone in your family die?"

"No, this card is for Barbara." I grabbed the card and put it back inside the plastic bag that it was in before she touched it. "She won't be able to make it tonight because she had a death in the family."

"Oh. That's a nice card…real nice message. But you're better than me because I can't see myself paying seven dollars for a greeting card. If it's more than four dollars, I put it back."

Why in the hell would you look at the price on the card? What a snoop, who does that?

Those questions ping-ponged around in my mind and were about to fly out of my mouth, but the doorbell sounded before I could part my lips.

"I'll get it," Caren said and sprang to her feet.

I stopped her by holding up my hand. "No, I'll get my own door. You just relax."

I could feel my blood pressure rising as I made my way to the front door. The gall to read a card that isn't for you, and then double down on the rudeness by checking the price on the back of it.

Lavern had no idea how much I wanted to grab her hand and run away with her when I opened the door.

"Hey!" Lavern shouted and greeted me with a love-filled hug. "Girl, I know I'm a little early, but I couldn't wait to see you! I brought wine!"

I looked back over my shoulder to make sure my shadow wasn't standing behind me, and then I mumbled, "Girl, you ain't nowhere close to being the earliest. As a matter of fact, your timing couldn't be more perfect."

Laverne entered with her normally bubbly attitude. She was the most pleasant person I know. Always had a positive outlook on life. The quintessential "glass half full" type of person. When she rounded the corner, she saw Caren sitting at the table. The two had never met, but Laverne had heard me complain about Caren before so she might have felt like she knew her intimately.

"Hi, I'm Laverne."

"I'm Caren."

"Y'all sit down and let's eat."

"Shoot, I'm full. I already pigged out," Caren said. "I'm just gon' sip on this wine."

"Girl, I'm starving. Give me whatever you got." Laverne looked around. "Is Barbara here?"

"No, she had a death in the family," Caren blurted out before I could respond.

"I'm sorry to hear that."

"Yeah, Beauty was telling me about it before you got here."

I wanted to scream *bullshit* but managed to keep the word corralled.

We managed to get through the first fifteen minutes without me strangling the life out of Caren. There were a couple of times when she rambled too long and caused Lavern to give me an odd side-eye look. But for the most part, the first fifteen minutes went smoothly. In hindsight, I should've ended the card game right then and kicked Caren out of my house the way Martin Lawrence used to do on his sitcom, *Martin.*

By nine o'clock we were popping the cork on our second bottle of wine. That's when I noticed something—Caren was dominating the conversation and she seemed to be in competition with Laverne. It's as if she was trying to prove to Laverne that she was a closer friend to me than Lavern was. In hindsight, I can blame Laverne for the atmospheric shift that night. She innocently asked Caren how she first met me. That's when the flood gates opened and refused to close.

"We've been knowing each other since college. Ain't that right, Beauty?"

I nodded and took my time swallowing the wine in my mouth.

"Oh, really? I didn't know that."

"Yeah, girl, we go waaaay back. We first met at the University. After college, we decided to move into this neighborhood to be around each other."
I held up a finger. "Actually, I moved in this neighborhood first, remember?"

"That's right. My husband and I had been looking for a house and we decided it would be cool to move over here after we saw how nice this neighborhood was. Before we could close, I saw another house I liked a few blocks away. We ended up buying that one."

I could feel my nerves getting worse, so from that point on, I drowned myself in wine to keep from issuing her a tongue lashing. But that didn't stop my flippant responses from swimming in my head every time she lied.

Bullshit. Your deal for the house on this block fell through. Y'all moved a few blocks away out of desperation because you couldn't qualify for anything else.

"Did Beauty tell you she's my daughter's godmother?" Caren asked.

"No," Laverne said with a hint of surprise in her voice. "Beauty and I talk a lot, but she never mentioned that to me. I'm surprised to hear it."

I avoided eye contact with Laverne because I knew she was mocking me.

"Yeah, she's my baby's godmother."

Tell her how you begged me to do it even though we were never that close.

"Yeah! I was supposed to christen Myra, but some kind of way our schedules got messed up."

No, they didn't. I told you I'd already found someone else to be my daughter's godmother.

"We became closer when Beauty took that buyout at General Motors and became a certified housewife."

How you just gon' put my business in the street? How do you know if I ever told Laverne about my buyout? Lord, please stop me from choking this woman.

Caren looked at me and held up her hand for a high-five. I'm not sure if it was the wine or my emotions taking over, but it felt like it took me an hour to raise my hand to slap hers.

"Do you remember at your retirement party that Kevin told you how I got in that big argument with that woman who wanted to sit next to you?"

For the record, you started that argument because you were mad that you weren't sitting next to me. As a matter of fact, you complained the whole night about the seating arrangements.

"Yep, I was there when he gave her that beautiful gold and diamond bracelet. Have you seen Beauty's bracelet?"

"No, I haven't," Laverne said.

"It is gorgeous. Beauty, I'm surprised you haven't shown her the bracelet."

Maybe because it ain't none of her damn business what kind of bracelet my husband bought me.

Laverne dug inside of her purse and pulled out her cellphone. She stared at the screen for a second and then shook her head.

"Beauty, I'm sorry honey, but I've got to go. Frank is texting me talking about he needs me to come home—it's an emergency."

"Oh, I hope everything is alright," Caren said.

Laverne waved dismissively. "I'm sure it is. I'll probably get there and what he wants wasn't even worth texting me about it. Y'all know how needy these men are."

"Girl, I know what you mean," Caren said. "Mine acts like he loses his mind if I'm out of his sight for ten minutes."

"Well Caren, it was nice meeting you."

"It was nice meeting you too," Caren said, "Next time we can get together at my house."

"Un-huh," Laverne grunted and made her way over to me. "Beauty, I'm sorry I've got to leave early."

"That's okay. I hope Frank is okay."

"If it's something bad I'll call you."

"Speaking of calling, let me give you my phone number," Caren said.

"Oh, I'll just get it from Beauty."

"Oh…okay. Well, you take care."

"You too."

"I'll walk you to the door," I said. As Laverne stepped outside, I grabbed her arm and whispered, "Heffa, I know you're lying."

Through pressed lips Laverne said, "I had to lie to get the hell out of there. That jackass was giving me a headache."

"Please don't leave me here with her," I pleaded in a voice loud enough that Laverne could here.

Laverne struggled to contain her laughter. The struggle was so real for her that she had water in her eyes when she pulled me in for a hug and whispered, "Beauty, that bitch really is crazy. I'm gon' pray for you."

"Please don't leave me alone with her." I refused to release my grip. "I'll pay you stay."

"Girl, you can't pay me enough to stay here and listen to her talk for another hour." Laverne broke free. "I'm gon' call you tomorrow and check on you." She was about to turn and walk away, and then turned back and pointed her finger at me. "And if you give that psycho my phone number, I'll never speak to you again."

I waved at Laverne as she backed away. She flashed a wide grin and blew me a kiss. I was on my own. After I closed the door, I rested my head on it and thought to myself, *I'm going to kill Kevin when he gets back here tonight.*

Chapter Seven

After a day of dark menacing skies, the clouds grumbled and roared around three o'clock in the afternoon. I'd already picked Myra up from school. KJ, who was entrenched and loving his routine of riding home with my neighbor, walked in the door a few minutes before four o'clock. No sooner than the door slammed behind him, those bruised clouds unleashed enough rain to make me consider building an arc.

I gave KJ the obligatory hug, which he quickly shrugged off the way all little boys his age does and made a beeline to his bedroom.

"Do not turn on that video game until after you do your homework!"

"I'm not, mama!"

I went into the kitchen to check on the pot roast I'd prepared and was whipping up a batch of Kool-Aid when Myra came skipping into the kitchen. She wrapped those twigs she called arms around my leg and then looked up at me with those big droopy eyes of hers that always made me melt.

"Mama," she whispered, "KJ in the room playing his video game."

"Myra, how many times have I told you not to be a tattle-tale?"

"A lot."

"So, why do you keep tattling?"

Myra's thick eyelashes flapped like a fan made of feathers. She flashed a quizzical look at me, shrugged, and said, "I don't know."

I took her beautiful face into my hands and kissed her forehead. I could still smell the lavender lotion that I'd slathered on her before taking her to school that morning.

"I'll deal with your brother, but I want you to stop tattling for little things. You can tell me if it's something real serious, but don't tattle for the little things."

"Okay. Is playing with the video game serious?"

"It is today," I said. I grabbed her shoulders and forced her to do an about face. With a playful pat on her butt, I said, "Now go get washed up. We're going to eat dinner as soon as your dad comes home."

"When is he coming home? I'm hungry."

"Soon," I said and peeked at my watch.

Truth of the matter was that I wasn't quite sure when Kevin would walk through the door. There had been a time when I knew his schedule so well that I could set my watch to it. But that changed once he got his promotion and new set of responsibilities. He'd be home by four one day and then six the next. He'd even walked through the door after ten o'clock one night. When I asked him why his schedule had become so unpredictable, he looked at me with lazy eyes and said, 'Mo' money, mo' problems, Babe,'.

As much as Kevin odd hours grated my nerves, I couldn't deny that the twenty-thousand dollars a year spike in his salary wasn't appreciated. It was because of his promotion, and subsequent pay raise, that I was able to be a stay-at-home mother. So, if having to play the guessing game with Kevin's schedule was the price that I had to pay for the new car he bought me and the ability to stay home and be a more hands-on mother, then so be it.

I lifted the lid on the pot roast that I had been babysitting and stabbed at it with a fork to check the tenderness. I hope he comes home while it's nice and warm. After rewarding my nostrils by taking an exaggerated sniff of the scent, I closed the lid, adjusted my game face, and marched straight to KJ's room.

KJ's bedroom door flew open and entered like the FBI with a warrant. With my fists bald and propped on my hips, the only thing that would've made me look more like a superhero was a cape. KJ's eyes—which were identical to his sister's—became as wide as his tv screen. His mouth formed a hole, but nothing came out. His words were obviously hiding—the way he would've if he could.

"Put. That. Remote. Control. Down." My arm shot out like an arrow in the direction of his book bag on the bed. "Pick up that book bag, and you'd better beat me to that kitchen table."

KJ grabbed the book bag and tucked it under his arm pit like a football. He scurried past me with his shoulders hunched as if he anticipated being smacked upside the head. He moved too swift for me to connect with his head, but I was able to give his shoulder a good hard smack that I was confident would sting enough to make him ease onto the kitchen table chair rather than plop down on it.

I shook my head frustratingly and watched my hardheaded son from his room to the kitchen table and then I yanked the video game plug out of the wall outlet. Like a cowboy strapping up the heels of a fallen calf, I wrapped the cord around the PlayStation with lightening quickness. I then tucked it under my armpit in the same manner that KJ grabbed his book bag, and then I strolled over to my bedroom and put it in the top of my closet.

Don't wanna listen to me? I'll show 'em. He'll get this sucker back when I get good and ready.

KJ and I engaged in a stare down that would've put western gunfighters to shame. I'm not sure what kind of names he was calling me in that little head of his, but I know they were bad because he was wise enough to cuss me with his eyes.

"I know you'd better stop looking at me like that lil' boy. When I tell you no video games before homework, I mean it."

"Can I have it back once I finish my homework?" he asked meekly.

"You can have it back when I feel like giving it back!" I barked. "Now, put your eyes on that paper and don't look up until your homework is done. And I'm *gon'* check it!"

I punctuated my answer with an eye roll and then went back to my pot roast. Before I could lift the lid and check on it again, the house phone rang.

"Hello."

"Oooh, somebody dun' made you mad!"

It was Caren. I could feel another eye roll coming on.

"Oh, hey Caren."

"You alright?"

"I'm fine. I just had to remind *somebody* who's the parent and who's the child around here!"

I glared at KJ. To his credit—and health—he kept those big eyes of his glued to his math homework assignment.

Caren chuckled. "Child, I understand. Mine be driving me crazy sometimes too."

Most people would've gaged from my tone and comment that they caught me at an awkward moment and probably this was not the time for casual conversation. But Caren wasn't *most* people. She had the emotional intelligence of a lamp post. Instead of bidding me ado, she segued into another conversation.

"So, how is KJ making out getting rides from school with your neighbor?"

I found the question odd, but no odder than some of the other stuff she'd asked me over the years like, which type of detergent I used? or, what time of the day did I prefer to cook dinner? Or the oddest, how many times a month did Kevin and I have sex? To which I replied in the snarkiest tone I could conjure, "Enough that you don't need to be concerned."

Still brooding from my exchange with my disobedient son, I shot a fire-filled gaze at him and answered without thinking, "He's enjoying getting a ride home with his friends, but I'm not sure how long I'm going to let that go on since he seems to have forgotten what he's supposed to do once he gets home from school."

KJ eyes looked up at me and quickly went back to his homework.

"Look Caren, I hate to be short, but I've got to get dinner finished up before Kevin gets home."

"Kevin hasn't made it home yet? Hmph. Well, okay. Call me when you get a chance."

"Yeah, I'll do that."

I hung up before she could get a chance to ask another weird who gives a damn question. I was so eager to get off the phone that I didn't pay much attention to the "Hmph" Caren managed to slip into her remark. In hindsight, I should have given it more thought. The kids and I ate dinner roughly thirty minutes later. Kevin's place at the dinner table was empty because he didn't come home that night until close to ten o'clock.

Chapter Eight

Our mail carrier dropped off the mail every day at around noon. He was a loud talking flirty man, with coffee-stained teeth and always smelled like a carton of cigarettes, so as was my routine, I waited until he was a few houses away before I went to the mailbox and grabbed the mail. While thumbing through the stack of bills, credit card solicitations, and various forms of junk mail, I noticed a gold envelope. My name was written in bold black letters on the cover.

That's odd; there is no name or return address on this, I thought. *It's not my birthday. I haven't done anything worthy of celebrating. Who would be sending me a letter?*

The scent of pasta waffled out of my house when I opened the front door. The kids requested spaghetti and meatballs that morning before they left for school, so I decided to whip up a batch. Truth be told, I was happy they requested spaghetti and meatballs because it was easy and fast to prepare.

I tossed the mail that I didn't want into the garbage can, pausing long enough to lift the lid on the pan with the salsa to make sure it wasn't burning, and then sat at the kitchen table. The gold letter was calling me. Whoever chose that color envelope knew what they were doing because it got my attention and captivated my curiosity.

I opened the seal slowly, as if there might be anthrax inside it. I recalled recently seeing stories on the news about anthrax being sent anonymously to people.

Beauty, you don't have any enemies, I told myself. *And even if you do have a few people out there who don't like you, they probably aren't mad enough to try to poison you through the mail.*

The letter was folded in three parts. I opened it and saw a typed letter. Once I started reading the letter, I got the shock of my life:

Beauty, you know you are really something, or else you think you are. You have a new car in your garage, but you have other people driving your child back and forth to school.

69

That's just tired, trifling, and sad. You should be ashamed of yourself. From now on, take your own child to school. By the way, you were not a good teacher that is why you are not teaching now. Oh, and one last thing...your husband is going out with a white woman. If you do not believe it, just go to the bar, and see for yourself.

"Oh my, God," I mumbled. "Someone sent me a poison pen letter."

Have you ever heard the phrase "time stood still"? Well, let me tell you something, at that moment, it wasn't just a figure of speech or cliché. At that moment, I felt like everything around me came to a screeching halt. The second hand on my wall clock froze. The steam seeping from the lid of my spaghetti sauce stopped in mid-air. Even the actors on *Young and the Restless*, my favorite daytime soap opera, stopped talking and looked like mannequins on my television screen.

The impact of what I read hit me like a freeze ray. I could feel myself moving, but it felt like I was moving in slow motion. My feet were sinking in emotional quicksand. I staggered over to the sofa on legs that were weaker than the spaghetti I was preparing for my kids to eat. I could feel my hands trembling, even the letter I held rattled from the vibration, but when I looked at my hands, I only saw a slight shimmy.

My mind drifted off to a place I dared not let it travel before. Images of Kevin leaving home carrying a backpack. When I asked him why he was toting it he told me it was filled with workout clothes that he'd put on when he went to the gym. I didn't question it. Why would I? Kevin hadn't lied to me before, so there was no need to think twice about his explanation. But with the whistleblowers comment ping-ponging around in my head, I couldn't help but revisit Kevin's excuse.

I do the laundry every week. Now that I think about it, I never saw any workout clothes in the dirty clothes hamper. But, when I went to take our clothes to the drycleaners, I did notice that his white Hugo Boss shirt that I bought him last Christmas wasn't in the closet. Nor were his brown slacks. Is that what he had tucked away in his backpack?

I looked at the letter again and reread it. This time I focused on the comment regarding my son getting a ride every day from the neighbor.

Why would anyone care about that? I'm his mother, if me or Kevin don't have a problem with KJ getting a ride from the neighbor, no one else should have anything to say about it. Maybe Pete's wife Lue sent this. She and I have a cordial relationship, but I wouldn't call us close friends. Maybe she secretly despises the fact that her husband is spending so much time with my son. Maybe this is her way of getting me to end the car-riding situation.

My eyes were as wide as the headlights on my car at this point. I could feel the surge of energy coursing through my limbs again. My fingers gripped the letter. My toes wiggled in my shoes. The thumping sound of my heart reverberated in my ears. The second hand on the clocks started to move. Victor Newman, my favorite character on *Young and Restless*, started to move on my television screen and I could hear his sinister, yet seductive, voice.

I looked at the letter one last time before tossing it aside. This time, my eyes zeroed in on the part about me not being a good teacher.

Why would this person say this? I was a damn good schoolteacher. I'm not teaching anymore because I chose to leave that profession. Wait...wait one minute. Not many people here even know about my former career as a schoolteacher. It's possible that Pete told Lue, but he doesn't know enough to comment on my performance; therefore, she wouldn't know enough about my life as a teacher to say this. The only other person that I can think of who knows enough about my past to even fix her mouth to say this is...

The telephone rung. I wasn't sure how long it had been ringing because I was in that momentary trance. Zombie-like, I walked over to the wall-mounted phone in the kitchen and answered it.

"Hello," I said robotically.

"Hey, babe. I called a couple of times over the last five minutes. The phone just kept ringing. Are you okay?"

"I'm fine," I mumbled. "I...I was in the bathroom."

"Oh. Well, I was just calling to let you know that I'll be home late tonight."

My eyes immediately drifted to the letter and latched on to the line about Kevin: *Your husband is going out with a white woman. If you do not believe it, just go to the bar, and see for yourself.*

"Really?"

"Yeah. The boss asked me to stay late to attend an emergency meeting."

"How long are you going to be?"

"Ain't no tellin'. You know how these meetings can run long sometimes."

"You've been having a lot of long meetings after work lately."

"That's true. I told you that was one of the downsides of the job. When you move into management you got to work longer than everyone else. That's why they put us on salary; to stop us from complaining whenever they keep us here after hours. Ain't nothin' I can do about that. As long as I accept their paycheck, I've gotta do what comes with it."

"Late night meetings."

"Yep. Late night meetings." Kevin waited a beat before he snaked off the phone. "Babe, someone is trying to get my attention. I've gotta go. I should be home tonight around ten."

Kevin hung up before I could say goodbye. If I didn't know any better, I would have thought the call was disconnected. But I did know better. He was in a hurry to end it before I could ask questions; questions that would force him to further explain the lie he'd concocted.

It was at that moment that my blinders came off. I discarded them the way a child discards a candy wrapper once the treat has been plucked from it. Regardless of the malicious intent of the person who'd sent the poison pen letter to me, she was accurate in her assertion. Notice I used the pronoun "she" to describe the sender. I used that pronoun because although I had no proof, I knew in my gut who'd sent the nasty letter to me. It was a person whom I'd known for years. A person whom I'd witnessed deliberately hurt others. A person who was fixated on my life. It was Caren.

By the time the kids made it home from school, I'd had a few hours to ponder my next move. I couldn't accuse Caren of sending the letter because I didn't have any proof. I couldn't show it to Kevin because he'd been excoriated in it too. I couldn't tell any of my friends about it because I was too embarrassed to talk about it. Kevin and I were the couple that other couples admired because we seemed to have it all together—or so I thought.

While Myra and KJ ate their dinner, I went into the home office determined to fight fire with fire. I retrieved an old typewriter from the top of the closet, plopped down in the chair, placed the typewriter on the desk, and pulled out a sheet of paper from the drawer.

KJ stuck his head inside the office.

"Mama, I'm finished eating dinner, and I have finished my homework. Can I play my PlayStation for a little while?"

I glance at the clock. It was 7:47 PM.

"You can play until eight thirty. After that I want you to take your bath and get ready for bed. If I come in there at eight thirty-one and you're still playing that PlayStation, I'm gonna take it again. Do you understand me?"

"Yes, ma'am."

KJ closed the door quickly. It reminded me of how fast his father hung up the phone after he informed me of the surprise "meeting" he had to attend. That fleeting thought brought me back to the task at hand. I was about to type my own poison pen letter.

Beauty, you know you shouldn't do this, that voice of reason whispered into my ear. *You're better than this...you're better than her.*

There are times in our life when we know the difference between right and wrong. God has supplied us all with discernment. The voice inside my head was telling me to calm down. It insisted that I back away from the typewriter before I did something stupid.

Unfortunately, there are also times in life when ego, super ego, are overridden by our id. Although we know we should listen to the voice of reason in our heads, we ignore and charge forward with our devious plans. This was one of those times for me.

I used Crazy Caren's letter as my template. I used similar words and the same ominous tone:

Caren, you know you are really something...or at least you think you are. With snake in the grass friends like you nobody needs any enemies. Do not ever come around me or my family again.

When I finished typing, I ripped the paper from the typewriter like an old school reporter who'd just finished typing a hot story and studied it to make sure it mirrored the letter she sent to me. I was determined to follow her example to the tee.

I grabbed a business envelope and stuck it into the typewriter, typed her name on it because I didn't want to write on the letter. Visions of a handwriting expert examining the letter and tracing the penmanship back to me flooded my mind. After I finished typing her name on the envelope—with no return address on it just like the one I received—I shoved the three-part folded letter inside of it.

Beauty, you really need to take a moment and think about this, the voice of reason whispered softly into my ear. *I know you're mad—you have a right to be. But too wrongs don't make a right. Besides, you still do not have concrete proof that Caren sent that poison pen letter to you. What if you send this anonymous letter to her and it turns out she's not the person who sent the original letter to you? How will you explain your actions to anyone: your kids, your husband, or even Caren? You'll go from being a sympathetic figure to a villain. I swatted away the thought like Serena Williams swats a tennis ball. I opened the top drawer on the desk and retrieved a postage stamp.*

The voice of reason was as pesky as a fly. It reappeared in my head.

Okay Beauty, hear me out. Before you mail this letter to her at least cover yourself by making sure you've explored all avenues. You don't want to put yourself in a position where you end up with egg on your face. You should take the letter she sent you to the police station and report it. Maybe there is something they can do to help—file a report, lift her fingerprints off it, something. At least you'll be able to sleep easily knowing that you tried everything before you did something as drastic as what you're planning to do.

As much as I hated to admit it, the voice inside of my head was absolutely right. I was reacting, not responding. A proper response would've been to report the threatening letter to the proper authorities and get instruction from law enforcement on what to do.

A deflating sigh hissed from my mouth. I was emotionally drained. What made me feel even more morose was the fact that I intuitively knew that this was just the beginning of a chain of events that would shake me to my core and turn my world upside down.

I sat in that chair pondering my next move longer than I planned. I looked at the clock and it read 8:37 PM. I was supposed to burst into KJ's room and catch him playing that PlayStation, but there I was, fighting back tears and trying to will the contents of my stomach to stay down while I tried to decide whether to ignore the poison pen letter I received or send my own. In the end, I settled on a compromise. I packed up the typewriter and put it back inside the closet. I tidied up the office desk to make it look like I'd never sat there. I tucked the letter I'd typed into my back pocket and muttered, "I guess I'll be going to the police in the morning."

Chapter Nine

By the time I awakened the next morning, Kevin was already gone for work. I immediately went into the closet and searched for his backpack. I found it tucked in the back corner. The only thing in it was a pair of socks and a t-shirt. I sniffed the t-shirt and it still smelled of the detergent and fabric softener that I used on all our clothes, so I know it hadn't been worn.

I made my way to the laundry and tossed the contents of the dirty clothes hamper the way a Correctional Officer tosses an inmate's cell. By the time I finished rummaging through the hamper there were so many clothes strewn around the laundry room that it looked like my washing machine and dryer had both vomited.

In the end, I didn't find what I was looking for—signs of infidelity: a shirt with lipstick on the collar; a t-shirt that smelled like a fragrance I didn't wear; or a pair of underwear with the scent of an essence other than mine on it. I found nothing. Zip. Zero.

You know the old sayin'…if you go looking for trouble, you gon' find it, said my inner voice.

"Shut up!" I barked, as if the inner voice had taken the form of a human and was standing next to me.

I was not in the mood to hear any reasoning. My previous day ended with me glancing at the clock on my nightstand, and seeing 10:47 PM in big red numbers, when Kevin tried to slide into bed without waking me. He turned his back and we slept in that back-to-back position all night; neither of us moving a muscle. Our feet didn't touch. There was no spooning. It was like an invisible barrier had formed between the two of us.

In many ways, a barrier had developed. It broke through the soil and rose as high as the wall former President Trump had built at the U.S. border. He'd emotionally cut me out of his life. And as I lay there in the darkness with my eyes wide open while I thought about that stupid poison pen letter, I received that exposed his infidelity, I realized that I'd begun the emotional process of blocking him out of my life. Our reluctance to touch each other was simply the manifestation of how we both felt. Kevin's body was there with me, but his mind was clearly on the other side of town. My body was there with him, and my mind was on the poison pen letter…and various ways of how to kill him and get away with it.

KJ hit me with another drive-by hug on his way out the door to catch his ride with Pete. I had so many things swirling in my mind that I didn't bother to force him to hug me correctly the way I normally would. I kissed his forehead, pinched his cheek, and let him leave.

My tattletale baby girl was in full effect, snitching like an FBI informant.

"Mama."

"Yes, honey."

"Guess what KJ did."

"Myra, what have I told you about tattling?"

"You told me to stop being a tattletale."

"Un-huh. And what are you doing right now?"

"I'm not tattling."

"Well, what do you call it?"

"I'm just telling you what I saw KJ do."

"Isn't that tattling?"

"No…because you told me I could tattle if I saw KJ do something that might get him into big trouble."

I pegged Myra as a Defense Attorney when she became an adult. That girl could talk her way out of a shark's mouth if given enough time. I had to admit, she made a good point. I did offer that one caveat to my "no tattling" rule, and my beautiful baby girl was cashing in her lottery ticket.

"Go ahead, Myra. What did you see your brother do?"

"He took two Pop Tarts out the box and put them in his book bag."

"You sure it was two?"

"Un-huh. I know because I saw him."

"Does he know you saw him?"

"Un-huh. He put his fist in my face and said he was going to beat me up if I told you."

"Well, you clearly ain't worried about getting beat up," I mumbled to myself.

"You gon' punish him, mama?"

"Don't worry about what I'm going to do to your brother. You just go get in the car so you can go to school. I'll be out in a second."

I grabbed my keys, purse, and the poison pen letter, and headed out to the car. I dropped Myra off at school and then made a beeline for the police station located roughly five miles from my house. The stop and go morning traffic created by school zones, teens on their phones while driving, and fender benders caused by folks so eager to go to work that they become raving lunatics on the road, made my drive twenty minutes longer than it should've been. Why is that important? Because an idle mind is the devil's workshop. And while I sat at those red lights, waited for crossing guards to wave me through the intersection, and slowly drove past angry motorist arguing while exchanging insurance information, I was tempted to go to Kevin's job and slap him and his Caucasian concubine in the face.

The police officer at the desk was sipping a cup of coffee when I approached the desk. I must've been wearing my emotions on my sleeve because he caught whiff of my energy the moment I burst through the door.

"Good morning, ma'am," he said as he hurriedly put down his coffee cup. He didn't know it yet, but the first time he looked in the mirror he was going to see a fresh coffee stain on the front of his uniform shirt. "How may I help you on this fine day?"

"You can help me by telling me what to do with this?"

My arm shot out from my side with the poison pen letter in my hand. It was crumpled at the edges, but he could still make out the nasty message. The officer rubbed his mid-twenties chin and then rubbed the back of his neck. I wasn't sure if he was searching for the right words or in desperate need of a bath. Either way, my patience was running thin.

"Well," I said angrily, "tell me what to do!"

"Well ma'am, this is definitely stalker behavior. If I, were you the first thing I'd do is be on high alert for any strange noises around my house or any signs that someone other than yourself, or someone you authorized, has been lurking around your house?"

"What kind of evidence?"

"You know like, footprints in your flower beds, around your windows, or on the concrete."

The thought of someone peeking in my windows sent chills up and down my spine.

"Whoever typed this has a real deep-seated issue with you."

"Tell me about it."

"The process of sitting down and writing a letter is time consuming. Was this left at your door, or did it get delivered via the mailman?"

"Mailman."

"So, this person had to go out and drop it off at the post office or at a mailbox."

"She could've just put it in her own mailbox."

"Could've, but I doubt it. If you were doing something this scandalous, would you mail it from your house where even the mailman would know it came from you?"

"I guess not."

"Nah, this person dropped this off somewhere to be mailed. Heck, a lot of people don't even want to go mail their bills. This person was determined to get this message to you." He put the letter on the desk. "You said "she" mailed it. Do you know who this came from?"

"I think I do. If I give you her address, can you guys go and talk to her?"

"I'm afraid not, ma'am."

"Why not?"

"Because for starters, you aren't sure the person you suspect is the actual sender."

I immediately thought that voice in my head the day before encouraging me to calm down and not doing something irrational.

"Secondly, you haven't been harmed."

"What do you mean! I just—"

The officer held up his hand. He'd clearly seen this type of case before and knew exactly what I was about to say.

"This letter is threatening, but it's not enough for us to round up the swat team."

"I'm not asking you to do that. I'm just asking if you can send some officers to her house to ask her some questions. You know…scare her a little."

"That's called harassment ma'am," he said condescendingly and handed the letter back to me.

"So, something has to happen to me before I can get help from law enforcement?'

"Something more than that letter."

"You look kind of young. Can I speak to your sergeant or someone in charge?"

"You can, ma'am, but he's going to tell you the same thing."

The officer spun cockily on his heels and sauntered toward the back of the building where a row of offices was located. Moments later, he returned with a tall barrow chest man following close behind him.

"I'm Sergeant O'Connor. How can I help you, ma'am?"

I gave him the letter. He read it and then asked without looking up, "Is this all you've got?"

"What more do I need?"

"More than this for our officers to act on it, ma'am. Maybe you should swing past the post office and ask to speak to the Postmaster. Maybe he can tell you what the rules are for flagging unwanted mail like this."

"I called the Postmaster already."

"What did he say?"

"It was a wasted phone call. He said they couldn't do anything because there were not threats in the letter. Their advice was to not read them and throw them away. That doesn't make sense to me because if I don't read them how will I know if there was a threat or not?"

The police officer shrugged. He had no good advice for me. I looked to the right of the large man and saw the young officer struggle to hide his smirk. I became more frustrated than I was when I got there. I snatched the letter off the desk and shoved it into my purse.

"Forget it. I'll handle this myself."

I stomped out of that police station like a spoiled child who'd been told she couldn't get a new toy. If the police weren't going to help me, I knew exactly what I was going to do—help myself.

Chapter Ten

When Kevin came home from work that evening, I waited until the kids had gone to bed and then I explained what happened throughout the day. I guess I expected some support from him, but what I got was his typical dismissive response.

"I just can't believe she sent it. I mean, she is weird acting, and I know she's done some questionable things to other people you know, but this seems a little too crazy, even for her."

The rage that surged through my body earlier when Caren was at my house resurfaced. Did he think I was just making this up? Did he think I wrote the letter to my damn self? Or maybe he thought this was some kind of sick attempt by me to get his attention. What bothered me the most by his reaction was that even if he wasn't fazed by her badgering me, he should've been outraged by the accusation that he was having an affair with a white woman, but that part of the letter he just glossed over. His lack of a comment about that claim didn't go unnoticed by me.

Rather than go back and forth with him about the letter and what Caren was capable of, I decided to back away from the discussion. Never had I felt so alone. He was my husband. He was supposed to support me. But all he seemed interested in doing was looking for reasons why Caren couldn't have been the person who sent it. Hell, by the time we finished talking he had me questioning myself. Did I overreact? Had I falsely accused Caren? I didn't have any proof she sent it—even the police officers told me that. But I could hear her voice as I read it. People write as they speak. I knew that I needed more time to think about it all. So, I left the matter alone and went to sleep.

That next morning, I woke up thinking about the letter. After getting the kids off to school, I found myself alone with that nasty letter. Since the police didn't offer much help, I was left with figuring out how to handle the situation on my own. I brewed a pot of tea, which helped me relax, and pondered my options. The longer I pondered, the angrier I got. The audacity to send me a letter like that. The mean-spirited nature of it. Her only goal was to destroy my family. I couldn't let that slide. I had to fight back. So, that's what I did. The response I drafted was going out, and I was prepared to deal with the fall out.

It only takes a day for a letter to travel from one house to another via mail when the houses are less than six blocks apart. I knew Caren had received the letter. All I needed to do was wait to see what her next move would be. The wait didn't last long.

When my doorbell rang, I sprang from my seat like a boxer leaps off the stool when he hears the bell for the next round. The kids were at school, my husband was at work, and I was in full-kick ass mode. After taking a moment to gather my composure, I opened my door with a stone face, clinched teeth, and bald fists.

"Hey, Beauty, you got a second?"

"Yes," I said sternly.

I stepped back and allowed her to enter.

"I got this letter in the mail yesterday." She held up the letter. "Did you send it to me?"

The thing that bugged me the most about Caren is that she was sloppy with her cattiness. It's like she didn't stop to think that if she approached me with an "anonymous" letter she'd received, it would be a clear indictment of herself. Why would she come to me unless she knew she'd provoked it? I suspect she thought I would deny it, but I could tell by the shocked look on her face that my frank response threw her for a loop.

"I sure did," I said. "You sent me one, so I decided to return the favor."

"I didn't send a letter to your house. I would never do anything like that. I don't understand why you would suspect me. I've been nothing but a good friend to you. I consider you my best friend. Instead of attacking each other, we need to put our heads together to try and figure out who would be coming after us and why."

I can't remember the last time I've wanted to slap the taste out of someone's mouth the way I wanted to at that moment. She stood there and lied with a straight face.

"You know what Caren; it really doesn't matter to me. I've known you long enough to know that you are more than capable of doing something this devious. I've seen you hurt people and get away with it. I've even seen you laugh and brag about the mean-spirited things you've done to people who hadn't done anything to you."

"That's not true!"

"Yes, it is. Do you need me to start rattling off times when you attacked people for no reason?"

Before she could answer I rattled off four different incidents. All she could do is stand there and look silly.

"Beauty, this is crazy. We've been friends for too long to throw it all away behind something like this."

I stared at her the way a judge stares at a defendant begging for a lighter sentence. She could see from my steely glare that I wasn't going to go light on her. That letter warranted the death penalty for our so-called friendship as far as I was concerned.

That's when it happened—she started crying. I'm not talking about a whimper; I'm talking about the ugly cry. Her crocodile tears didn't move me. In fact, they made me angrier. I walked over to my front door, opened it, and stood there.

"If it turns out that I'm wrong about you sending that letter to me, I apologize, but my gut tells me that I'm not. I'm following my gut. And my gut is saying to stop dealing with you...in any way, shape, form, or fashion."

She'd made her move and I'd made mine. Caren was officially unfriended, and I was free to go on with my life...or so I thought.

Two days later, I went to my favorite nail salon to get my bi-weekly manicure. The technicians all knew me because I'd been going to them for so long. They were so familiar with me that they could sense my mood the moment I walked through the door.

"Come and sit," said Kim, the technician who did my nails the most.

After making small talk, Kim pivoted to a more disconcerting topic.

"Beauty, I want to tell you something."

"What's up?"

"Do you know a Caren Ring?"

"Yes, why?"

Although Kim's head was tilted downward while she worked on my nails, I could see ridges form on her forehead.

"Is something wrong?" I asked.

"I'm not sure. This Caren woman came in here asking questions yesterday."

A chill slithered down my spine. It felt like a centipede had somehow climbed inside of my shirt and was scurrying down to my waist.

"What kind of questions?"

"She wanted to know which technician you used when you came in."

"Oh, really. What else?"

"She wanted to know what color you use. And then she said something about scheduling her appointments on the same day you schedule yours. At first, we didn't think it was a big deal, but…"

"But what?"

"…I don't know. There was just something about her that was weird." Kim looked up at me. "You should be careful. She seemed obsessed with you."

Ironically, I had the poison pen letter Caren sent me in my purse.

"Kim, you're righter than you realize."

I showed it to Kim. She was almost as surprised as I was when I first received it. Kim's jaw dropped. She read it and then called over Sun-Li, the other technician who worked on my nails occasionally. They were both floored by what they read. Needless to say, I instructed them to not give any information about me to anyone. They shook their heads in agreement and promised to let me know if Caren returned and asked any more questions. For a split second, I pondered letting Kim know that I wouldn't be returning but decided not to. I was not about to let a crazy woman dictate where I could, and couldn't, go.

Later that week, I watched from my window as my creepy mailman placed a stack of mail inside of my mailbox and then walked away. Once he was a few houses away, I strolled to the mailbox. Per my normal routine, I sifted through the junk mail as I walked back to house. But I stopped abruptly when I saw it—another poison pen letter. Just like the first one, it didn't have a return address. But just like the first one, I knew exactly who it was from.

I scurried to the house, fumbling mail as I made my way, and ripped the letter open. I didn't even bother to sit down while I read it. The ink on this letter was red.

I guess she's pissed off, was my initial thought and then I read the letter.

Are you stupid? Don't send your son to ride with us. Take your son to school yourself. We are tired of taking him back and forth.

Needless to say, I was speechless. Rather than wait for Kevin to get home from work, I immediately called him at his office.

"Pete and Lue would never send a letter like that," Kevin said. "I've known Pete long enough to know that if he felt that way, he'd pull me to the side and tell me."

"I know that. I didn't for a second think Pete or Lue sent this. Lue is too sweet to do something like this. She and I have been friends since the day we met. And I consider Pete a friend too. This is not their style, but it is that dingbat Caren's style. She was busted pulling one of her little stunts. I called her on it, and now she's trying to shift attention away from herself and put it on our neighbors. Now, do you believe me when I say she's crazy?"

"Yeah, I believe you," he sighed and replied begrudgingly.

"Which leads me to another thing we need to discuss," I said.

"What?"

"The part of the first letter when she said you are seeing some white woman. What's up with that? Is there something you need to tell me?"

"Babe, you just said the woman is crazy."

"You still haven't answered me, Kevin."

"No, I don't have anything to tell you."

Right then, I could hear someone enter his office and ask him a question.

"Hey, I have to go. We can talk about this later."

I spent the rest of the afternoon cleaning up my house and cooking. I tend to do both when my nerves were frayed. And after receiving the second poison pen letter, my nerves were downright singed. It wasn't until KJ came through the door that I considered the domino affect the letter could have.

If this woman is so obsessed with me that she's still commenting on my son getting a ride to and from school, maybe she is watching my son when I'm not around. If she's lurking and leering to watch my son, that means the kids he hangs out with could be at risk. I need to discuss this letter with Pete and Lue.

"What's for dinner?" KJ asked.

"Spaghetti and meatballs."

"Again!"

"Boy, be quiet and start doing your homework!" I barked. "Watch your sister for a minute, I need to go talk to Mr. Pete."

"But you told me to do my homework."

"KJ, can you walk and chew gum at the same time?"

KJ thought about the question for a second and said, "Yeah!"

"Well, you can do your homework and keep an eye on your sister too."

Before he could say something flippant that could get him spanked and me answering questions from the Child Protective Services (CPS) office, I grabbed the second letter and marched across the street to Pete and Lue's house.

When I arrived across the street, Pete opened the door before I could ring the doorbell.

"Come on in," Beauty he said.

There was an air of anxiety in his voice. His facial expression matched his tone.

When I entered, I saw Lue sitting on their living room sofa.

"Hey, Lue."

"Hey, Beauty. I'm glad you came because we were about to come see you."

I felt a lump the size of a golf ball form in my throat. Had my worst fear come to pass? Did that crazy lady threaten their child?

"I came to talk to you guys about a letter I received."

Lue held up a letter. "That's the same thing we wanted to talk to you about."

"Someone sent us this anonymous letter," Pete said.

Lue handed the letter over to me. I could feel my blood boiling as I read it.

Why won't you all stop taking other people kids back and forth to school. They can take their own kids to school. You are stupid, you should let them ride their own kids around, they have a new car sitting in their garage.

Embarrassed isn't a strong enough word to describe how I felt. I was stunned! This crazy woman had gotten their address and sent them a letter to advert the blame from her.

"Guys, I am so sorry you had to get mixed up in this."

"Mixed up in what?" Pete asked.

I let out the loudest sigh ever and started recapping.

"I believe these letters were sent by a former friend of mine named, Caren. Honestly, I think she's crazy. I first met her back at the University. And then when we moved here, she followed. She even tried to buy a house on this block shortly after we bought one, but the financing didn't go through. She ended up buying a house a few blocks away. When I had my baby, she wanted one. When I got my new car, she went out and bought one. I get something new in my house, she goes out and buys something similar."

Lue's eyebrows rose like the arches on the McDonalds logo. She rubbed her neck like she was reaching for her imaginary pearls. Pete folded his arms and stared at me. I could tell from his facial expression that he was ready to grab his gun.

"Apparently, Caren noticed that KJ started to get rides back and forth to school with you, Pete. She never mentioned it to me because she knows I would've told her to mind her business. But the other day, I got a poison pen letter in the mail." I gave my letter to Pete and spoke directly to Lue. "She said I should stop letting KJ ride back and forth to school with you and that I should bring my child to school myself."

Pete gave the letter back to me. "How do you know for sure this "Caren: woman sent it?"

Because she's one of the few people who knows my real name. Like I said, we've known each other since college.

"She sounds like one of those crazy women on those Lifetime movies you be watching, babe," Pete said to Lue.

"Yeah, she does sound crazy," Lue said to me.

"Maybe you should go to the police."

"I did."

"What did they say?" Lue asked.

"Nothing. They basically told me I don't have enough proof that Caren sent it. And without solid proof they can't do anything."

"That's because you're black," Pete said and sat down. "If you were a white woman, they would've already hauled Caren in for questioning."

"You're probably right," I said with fire in my eyes. "Unfortunately, I ain't white. I've got to figure out what I'm gon' do. In the meantime, I'm going to bring KJ to school myself. I don't like the idea of him being watched. That means that she could be watching your child too and I don't want that on my conscious. I want to apologize for bringing this foolishness to your doorstep."

"No need for you to apologize," Pete said. "Caren is the crazy one."

When Kevin came home, I told him about my conversation with Pete and Lue.

"You did what?"

"I went and told them what was going on."

"Why?"

"Because they needed to know. I even showed them the letter."

"What letter?"

"The one Caren sent me."

"The first letter?"

I was confused by his question at first, but then it dawned on me why he was asking which letter I let them see. The first letter contained the accusation that he was cheating. That was the last thing he wanted anyone to read about.

I gave Kevin a few moments to ask more questions, but he didn't.

"I also told them that I'd be taking KJ to school from now on. I don't think it's fair to put their child in harm's way."

"You think she'd try to hurt the kids?"

"I don't know, but I don't wanna risk it. Besides, I'd feel more comfortable if I was there to protect my child."

"You mean our child," Kevin interjected.

"Yes…our child."

Our conversation was interrupted by the doorbell. I was about to go and open the door, but Kevin grabbed my arm, "I'll get it."

I remained in the bedroom while Kevin went to answer the door, but I could hear him greet Pete and Lue.

"Come on in," Kevin said.

"We're not staying long," Pete said.

I walked into the living room. "Hey. Is everything okay?"

"Oh, hey, Beauty," Lue said. "We just came over to tell y'all that we've thought a lot about the situation with this Caren woman. And—"

"We ain't having it!" Pete blurted out. "She can be crazy if she wants to, but she ain't running nothing over here. So, with that being said, we wanted to tell y'all that we are still willing to give KJ a ride to and from school for as long as we're picking up our own son. And to be honest with all that you all know, and what we learned about this crazy chic, I won't be able to sleep knowing she might be lurking around the school or this neighborhood. I *want* to keep bringing all the children."

"Are you sure?" I asked.

"Trust me," Lue said, "he's sure."

"That settles it," Pete said and opened the front door. "We expect to see KJ in the morning."

"He really is a great kid," Lue said.

"We feel the same about your son," Kevin said.

Our neighbors left. I felt better about the situation—all except the part about my husband and the white woman.

Chapter Eleven

T wo weeks passed before we had any more trouble out of Caren. The kids were being shuttled back and forth with no problem. Kevin and I seemed to be getting along better. He even started coming home from work in time to eat dinner with the family. Life was getting back to normal.

One afternoon, while helping KJ figure out a math homework problem, he said something that surprised me.

"Oh yeah, I forgot to tell you. Billie is in my class."

"Who?"

"Billie Ring…Ms. Caren's daughter. She transferred to my class."

"When did this happen?"

"The other day."

"Why did they put her in your class?"

KJ shrugged.

My mental wheels started spinning. Based on everything that had happened, I knew this couldn't have been a coincidence.

The next day, I told Pete I'd pick KJ up from school myself so that I could take him to his dentist appointment. When I arrived at school, KJ came to the car and told me that his teacher, Mrs. Smith, needed me to come and sign the Parent/Teacher Conference form.

I parked my car and went inside. It was after school and the hallways was sparse, other than a few teachers, scurrying to gather their things and leave for the day. I poked my head into KJ's teacher's class.

"Hi, Mrs. Smith. I'm Beauty, KJ's mother."

"It's so nice to see you," Mrs. Smith said. When she stood up, I thought I was looking at a giant. She was taller than my husband. "Yes, I played basketball in college."

"I'm so sorry." I didn't mean to stare.

To her credit, Mrs. Smith waved dismissively and smiled. "I'm used to it. You can't walk around at 6'6" as a woman and be surprised that other people are surprised to see you."

I was low-key envious of her. She was tall with curvy legs that seem to start at arm pits. She wore a short hairstyle that was tapered in the back. It looked like it had been plucked from a magazine. Her chocolate skin was flawless. If she hadn't played basketball, she would have been a great model.

"You are beautiful," I said, not even realizing I was about to say it. "Now I see why my son is always eager to come to school."

KJ blushed.

"Kevin is a wonderful child. And he's such a gentleman."

I looked down at KJ and said, "Close your mouth son, you're drooling."

I was only partially joking. She really was that pretty. I even made a mental note to never let his father come to any parent/teacher meetings. The idea of having both of my men crushing on Mrs. Smith, would be too much.

"KJ said you needed me to sign a Parent/Teach conference form."

"Yes. As you know the conferences are in two days. To make sure each parent gets enough time and attention to talk about their child, we're scheduling the meetings, giving every parent fifteen minutes. Please sign right here." She grabbed the clipboard. "This page is filled up, let me get a new page."

Mrs. Smith turned and walked back to her desk. The skirt she wore showed off a figure many women pay to get. I looked down and saw KJ staring at her butt and pinched his arm. He was still rubbing it and grimacing when she returned.

"Here we go. Just put your name here at the top. We have two time slots available: 6:00pm to 6:15pm or 6:30 to 6:45. Which would you like?"

"I'll take the 6:30 to 6:45 time," I said and filled in my name "Thank you.".

"It was nice meeting you." She looked at Kevin. "See you tomorrow, Kevin."

KJ stood there with a goofy grin plastered on his face. I nudged him to break his trance.

"Oh, umm, yes ma'am."

I rolled my eyes and looked at Mrs. Smith. "You see what you've done to my child."

Kevin and I were like a tag team in a wrestling match on the day of the conference. I'd already prepared dinner. The kids had already completed their homework and had eaten. And Kevin's plate was warming in the oven. We gave each other a peck as he entered, and I exited.

"I'm headed to the school to have a conference with KJ's teacher. The kids are straight, and your plate of food is in the oven."

When I got to the school it reminded me of a college campus when students are moving into their dorm rooms. Parents wandering around looking aimless. Kids huddled up in groups snickering and asking each other the same question: Is that your mama?

I set my sights on the entrance to Mrs. Smith's class and headed that way. When I was less than ten feet from the door, Caren stepped out of the classroom and into the hallway. I was surprised to see her, but she seemed as if she'd been waiting on me. It was the first time I'd been in her presence since I politely kicked her out of my house, so this was awkward to say the least.

"Hello, Beauty," she said in a voice tone that hovered just above a whisper.

I didn't respond. Mainly, because I couldn't guarantee that my response wouldn't be filled with expletives. Instead, I attempted to side-step her. But Caren wasn't having it. She moved in front of me and blocked my path.

"I just want you to know that I didn't send those letters to you."

While I stood there looking like I'd just been transported into an episode of the Twilight Zone, Caren slid past me and scampered down the stairs.

"Right on time," Mrs. Smith said and waved her arm at her classroom like a game show host showing off a new car. "Come on in."

On my drive back home, I spent more time thinking about running into Caren than Mrs. Smith's comments about KJ tendency to stare at her and the need for us to work with him more on his math.

She must've come in after me to sign up for the Parent/Teacher conference because she was leaving when I left out. She could have chosen a slot after me, but she took the slot right before me so that she could be there when I arrived. Now it's clear why she had Billie transferred into KJ's class. She is sitting around plotting encounters.

As I pulled my car into our driveway and waited for the garage door to open, another thought struck me like a bolt of lightning.

When we were in the hallway she said, 'I just want you to know that I didn't send those letters to you.' How in the hell would she know about the second letter unless she sent it? I didn't confront her about it.

As I entered the house, Kevin was sitting on the sofa watching ESPN.

"How'd the conference go?" he lazily tossed over his shoulder. His eyes—or attention—never left the television.

"It went okay. We need to work harder with KJ on his math and he has a crush on his teacher."

"All boys go through that. It's a rite of passage."

"Oh, something else interesting happened."

"What?"

"I ran into Caren."

That got Kevin's undivided attention. He grabbed the television remote control and lowered the volume on the television and looked at me.

"What happened?"

I grabbed a bottle of water and leaned on the kitchen counter.

"Nothing much other than she told me that she didn't write those letters."

"Letters," he repeated. "Did you confront again about the second letter?"

"Nope."

"So how does she know about the second letter?"

I pursed my lips and folded my arms.

Kevin nodded and said, "She knows about it because she's the one who sent it."

"Bingo!" I said and sipped my water.

"Well, she practically confessed. What are you going to do?"

"Take this to the next level."

Chapter Twelve

I'd never been to the city attorney's office, so I was shaking like a leaf on a tree during a hurricane when I walked into the building. The floors were shiny enough to eat off. Men and women walked past wearing business suits. They all had briefcases in one hand and their cellphones in the other. They all seemed so engaged in their phone calls and conversations about ongoing cases that I wondered if anyone would care about what I was dealing with.

Ironically, it was while watching an episode of my favorite daytime court television show that I got the idea to take my complaint to the city attorney office. I recognized that it was a long shot, but I was desperate to receive help from anyone at that point, so I decided to give it a shot.

I walked into Mike Greenwall's office expecting to be shown the door within five minutes, but nothing could have been further from the truth. He and his staff treated me like the most important person in the building. Their hospitality helped me relax. And once I became relaxed, I laid out my case like I should've been one of the folks walking around there in a business suit.

"I must admit, Beauty, you make a cogent argument," Mike said while he nodded his head. "You did a good job compiling the evidence."

"Is the evidence good enough for you to do something?"

"It's certainly good enough to justify us bringing her in for an interview."

I left Mr. Greenwell's office feeling like I was floating. It was the first time since the chaos started that I felt like someone heard me. Unfortunately, my feelings of euphoria only last a week.

One week after meeting with Mike Greenwell, I received a call from his office.

"This is Beauty."

"Hi, this is Mike Greenwell. Do you have a moment to talk?"

"Hi Mr. Greenwell!" I shouted. "I've been looking forward to your call. How's it going?"

"It's going," he said, with little enthusiasm. "Look, I won't take up much of your time. I just called to tell you that I interviewed Caren."

"She's crazy, huh?"

"Actually, I found her to be anything but crazy. I found her explanation of what took place to be very credible. She wasn't bombastic or rude. In fact, she conducted herself with style and grace."

I didn't have a mirror in front of me, but I'm sure that my face looked like I'd bitten into a grapefruit stuffed with spinach and drenched in apple cider vinegar.

"Excuse me."

"I spoke to Caren and asked her to explain the issues you brought to my attention."

"I'm sure she lied."

"Well, I can't speak to that, but she did bring up some things that you failed to mention."

"Things like what?"

"Like the fact that she confronted you about having an affair with her husband."

"What! That's a bold face lie!"

"Calm down, ma'am."

"Don't tell me to calm down. That woman has been stalking me. And even started harassing my neighbors. I showed you the proof and you looked me in my face and said I'd done a good job of compiling the evidence."

"Yes, I did say that. But that was before I spoke to Caren."

"You mean, before you let yourself get conned by her." I paused to take a deep breath. After a hearty exhale, I continued. "So does this mean you're not going to help me?"

"I would need something more blatant to happen. Right now, this is boiling down to a typical he said, she said."

I was so angry that I hung up without saying goodbye. It probably wasn't the wisest thing to do to the city attorney, but he'd insulted my intelligence and I wasn't having it.

Caren must have been feeling proud of the snow job she laid on the city attorney because she went to the stationary store and purchased three Sweetest Day cards for me, and my children then mailed them right off. How do I know? Because they came the day after she was brought in for her questioning. She had placed the date and time on the cards as well.

The emotional toll this was taking on me was something that I didn't notice, but apparently others did; in particular, my kids and husband. I was always somewhat of a neat freak and regimented person. I cleaned up in the same manner every day: kitchen, living room, bedrooms, and bathrooms. I started dinner at 2:00 PM so that it would be finished and ready to serve before my kids made it home from school. That was my routine. But it's hard to stick to a routine when your thoughts are elsewhere. And with each passing day, my thoughts lingered on what I would do if I found myself face-to-face with Caren.

Sometimes, the universe can be catty. It's like combustible situations are orchestrated so that higher powers can sit back, eat popcorn, and laugh. It's like we—the human race—are the characters in one big reality show and God and the angels are watching us and arguing about which characters are crazy, which character will toss a glass of water, and which character will be an antagonist and then play a victim.

I felt like I was in one of those reality television moments when my cellphone rang and it was Marsha, an old college friend.

"Heeeeyyy giiirl!" Marsha said in her typical sing-song voice. Back when we attended the University, she spoke that way and it drove me crazy because I thought it was an act. Twenty years later, she still talked that way, so I realized it wasn't. "What's up wit'cha?"

"Nothing," I sighed, hoping the fact that I was lying couldn't be detected. "I'm fine. How have you been."

"I'm fine, but you don't sound fine. You sound like someone just ran over your puppy. Are you okay?"

"No, really, I'm fine. Just a little tired that's all. What's up?"

"What's up?" Marsha replied indignantly. "What's up is the same thing that's up this time every year—our Christmas dinner."

With the chaos swirling around my family, I'd completely forgotten about the large couple dinner that Marsha and her husband, Monty, hosted every year.

"Actually friend, it did slip my mind."

"Are you and Kevin coming this year?"

"That depends."

"On what?"

"On whether Caren and Robert are invited."

"Yeah, they're invited. They come every year. Well, almost every year. What's going on?"

I really didn't want to put my business out in the streets, but Marsha was a dear friend and I felt like I should tell her the truth.

"We're kind of embroiled in a beef with Caren. She and I aren't friends anymore."

"What happened?"

"She's been sending me poison pen letters."

"Poison what?"

"You've never heard of a poison pen letter?"

"No. What is it?"

"It's a mean-spirited threatening letter designed to evoke anguish and suffering. sent anonymously."

"Why would she do that?"

"Your guess is as good as mine. She swears she didn't send it."

"Well, if it was sent anonymously, how do you know she's the sender?"

I swear, if I had a dime for every time someone asked me that question, I'd be rich.

"I just knew it was her from the things said in the letter and my gut. And then she all but told on herself when I confronted her."

"What happened?"

"Well, for starters, I've known Caren long enough that I can tell when she's lying."

"Yeah, she always was a terrible liar," Marsha said. "You remember that time in school when she almost got expelled for stealing that girl's term paper. And then swore up and down she didn't do it. We knew she was lying before she even admitted to us that she did it."

"Yeah, but she managed to talk her way out of getting put on probation by lying to the Dean."

"Yep. To this day I don't know how she pulled that off."

"She pulled it off because she's a damn sociopath. She's manipulative as hell and always has been. I reported her to the city's attorney office. They brought her in, and even with the proof I showed them, she managed to lie her way out of that too."

"Damn."

"Told the man that she believed I was messing with her husband."

"You're lying!"

"Child, I wish I was. By saying that foolishness it—"

"Was enough to cast doubt on your version because it made you look like you had an agenda."

"Exactly!"

"Damn she's good," Marsha said. "Beauty, I'm sorry you're having to deal with this."

"Me too," I said exhaustively. "So, now you know why I can't be in her presence. I can't promise you that all hell wouldn't break loose if we were in the same room and I don't want to ruin your beautiful event. I hope you and Monty understand."

"Of course, I do. And after I tell him what you just told me, I'm sure he'll understand too. So, if y'all ain't coming here for our party, what are you doing to celebrate Christmas?"

"Nothing much. I might go to Kevin's office party, but to be honest with you, I don't know if I even want to do that. I just feel like I need some *me time* to sort everything out."

"Trust me, I understand. Well, call me if you need someone to talk to."

"I will. Thanks for understanding."

"No problem. I love you."

"I love you too."

My doorbell rang shortly after I hung up the phone with Marsha. It was Pete with KJ standing next to him wiping his eyes.

"Hey, Pete." I looked at KJ and saw the dejected look on his face. "What's going on?"

"I think you should talk to KJ; he can tell you what happened. I just wanted to walk him across the street just to be safe."

Walk him across the street for safety. What in the hell is that supposed to mean?

"Oh, okay. Well...thanks."

I gently grabbed KJ by the shoulder and led him inside. We sat at the kitchen table.

"Tell me what happened."

"Me and a boy named, Malcolm, were chosen to go down and pay for the class popcorn and bring it to class to pass out. When we got to the gym where they were passing out the popcorn, I saw Ms. Caren."

"In the hallway?"

"No. She was working with the teachers passing out the popcorn."

"Oh, she was a volunteer."

"Yeah."

"So, what happened?"

"Mrs. Smith gave me the money to hold because Malcolm is always losing some of it. So, I was the one who had to pay for the popcorn. When I went to give Ms. Caren the money, she grabbed my hand and held it. And then she...she..."

"She did what?"

"She leaned down close to my face and said, 'I am not the one sending the letters.'"

"And then what happened?"

"She let my hand go and took the money."

"Are you sure it happened just like that?"

"Yeah. Malcolm saw what happened too. When we left the gym with the popcorn he just started laughing and teasing me and telling me I looked scared. I told him I was going to beat him up if he kept saying that."

"No, I don't want you fighting. I'm sure Malcolm didn't mean no harm." I smothered KJ with a motherly hug. I could feel his little heart racing when our bodies were pressed together. "Mrs. Caren and I are not friends anymore. The next time something like that happens I want you to tell Mrs. Smith or another teacher."

"What if no teacher is around?"

"Then you start yelling "stranger danger" and run away. I don't want you going anywhere near her anymore. Okay."

KJ nodded. I kissed his forehead.

"Okay. I want you to go into your room and start working on your homework. I'm not cooking today. I'm going to go and pick up your sister and then I'll stop and get some McDonalds."

The mere mention of McDonalds was enough to bring a smile to KJ's face.

"Do not open this door for anyone while I'm gone."

"What if Mr. Pete comes over?"

"I said no one. Do you understand me?" My tone must have been harsh because KJ froze and said, "Yes ma'am."

Once KJ went into his bedroom, I went into mine. I went into the room wearing a loose-fitting shirt, jogging pants, slippers, earrings, and my wedding ban. I came out of my bedroom wearing tight jeans, a tighter t-shirt, running shoes, and no jewelry. The smoke coming from my ears left a trail like a locomotive as I stormed out of my house.

I made it to Caren's block in record time. My tires squealed when I slammed on the brakes and hopped out. It still amazes me to this day how her front door didn't cave in from the way I slammed my first against it.

"Come out Caren!"

When my first request went unanswered, I banged even harder on the door.

"If you think you can put your hands on my child and nothing happens, you got another thing coming! Come outside so I can put my hands on you!"

Still there was no response. This cycle of banging and threats went on another five minutes, but Caren never came out. If it weren't for the threatening looks of a few of her neighbors and the fact that I knew I still needed to go and pick up

Myra from the schools after care program, I probably would've spent another thirty minutes camped outside of that vixen's front door.

I hopped back into my car and nearly broke my fingernail when I stabbed the speed dial button next to Kevin's name.

"Hello."

"You will never believe what that cow did."

"Who?"

"Caren!"

Kevin sighed. "What happened now?"

"She put her hands on KJ!"

"She did what?"

"You heard me. She put her hands on our son!"

"Is he okay?"

"Yes. But that's besides the point. She—"

"Wait, wait, wait...calm down. Did she hit him?"

"No."

"But you said she put her hands on KJ. Now you're saying KJ is okay."

"Yes, he is."

"Bae, you're not making sense. Start from the beginning."

"KJ came home upset. He told me that he saw Caren at the school giving out popcorn. He went to pay for the popcorn for his class. Caren grabbed his arm and told me that she didn't send the poison pen letters. So, no, she didn't hit him or curse at him, but she did scare the hell out of him. That's why I went to that cow's house."

"You what?"

"I went to her house."

"To do what?"

"To put my hands on her the way she put her hands on our child."

"Did she come out?"

"No. But I know she was in there. I waited for a while, but when her neighbors started coming outside, I left."

"Go home!"

"Why are you yelling at me?"

"Because you are about to make things worse than they already are. What if she calls the police? You can't be going around threatening people."

"But—"

"But nothing! Go home and stay away from that woman."

"I was defending our child, Kevin."

Kevin whistled another disgusted sigh. "Babe, a wise man said never argue with a fool, because from a distance people can't tell who the fool is. You may think you had a good reason to be there, but her neighbors are looking at you like you're crazy because now they see you as the fool."

Chapter Thirteen

Kevin and I didn't speak much after I went to Caren's house. He was annoyed because I went there, and I was annoyed at him for not supporting my decision. I walked into the kitchen and smelled the pot of coffee he was brewing. The aroma was soothing. I could feel a sense of relaxation coming over me just from the thought that I would be sipping a cup soon.

"Do you think you'll be able to make it to my office Christmas party this evening?"

"I doubt it," Beauty replied as she poured a cup of coffee. "I need to do some shopping and I still need to go out and buy something to wear to the

Holiday dance next week at the University. By the way, Marsha called me again and is begging us to come to her party. I told her about how we were trying to avoid Caren and she said it wouldn't be a problem because Caren ain't going."

"Sounds like you really want to go."

"Honestly, I do. I've been feeling trapped and smothered here lately. I need to get out and see some old friends. I think it would be good for us as a couple to go do something together. Do you mind if I tell her we're going to come?"

"I don't mind. I agree with you. You're going stir crazy being in this house every day—I can see it. I think the trip will do you some good. Yeah, tell her we'll come. The only thing that gives me pause is the Caren situation. I'm not sure if this is the wisest thing to do because we know there's a chance that Caren is going to be there. I'm not trying to be involved in a boxing match at a Christmas party."

"You make it sound like I can't control myself."

"You've proven that when it comes to Caren, you can't. That woman brings out a side of you that I never knew existed."

"All I want is for her to stay away from me and my family."

"Yeah, well...we've got to be better than her."

Kevin left abruptly. He used to give me a kiss before he left for work, but this time, he offered a lame forearm squeeze and left. Let's just call it a drive-by departure. I wanted to grab him, wrap my arms around his waist, and squeeze until that fire that used to burn between us was back. The passion that I could feel was evaporating like droplets of water on the hood of a car during the dead of summer.

I spent the first half of the day out shopping. I even managed to get to my nail tech to have my nails touched up. I was glad to hear that she didn't have anything to report regarding Caren coming around snooping. Ever since our first discussion about my stalker, the technicians were constantly on the lookout. She freaked them out just as much as she freaked me out.

When the kids came home, I helped them with their homework. I didn't bother cooking because it was a Friday. Instead, I ordered a large pepperoni pizza and let them have at it. I even told KJ he could stay up all night playing that game if he wanted to. I didn't care. The kids were in their own worlds. Kevin was at his company's office party, And I had my evening all mapped out. I intended to sip some wine and get trapped between the pages of a romance novel until I dozed off.

It was almost six o'clock and I was just starting the second chapter of the novel that I was reading when the phone rang.

"Hello," I said, a little annoyed that my "me time" had been disturbed.

"You ain't gon' believe this?"

"Kevin? Is that you?"

"Who else is it going to be?"

"You sound a little different. I didn't catch your voice."

"I probably sound different because I'm livid right about now."

"Why?"

"She came to my office."

"Who?"

"Caren!"

"What?"

"You heard me. That crazy woman just came to my office. She came here to tell me that she didn't write those poison pen letters. She kept telling me that I needed to believe her because she has always been a good friend to us, and she would never do anything to hurt us. She even went on and on about how the city attorney didn't even believe she did it."

I let Kevin talk until he got tired. I didn't interrupt him; I just listened.

"Hello! You still there?'

"Yeah, I'm here."

"Babe, I just told you that woman came to my job—making a damn scene in front of my employers and peers, and all you can do is just hold the phone?"

"Kevin, what do you want me to say? I've been telling you for months that Caren is not acting like a sane person. I told you she was evil. I even gave you example after example of it. First you didn't believe me. Then you basically told me to stay away from her although you knew that was damn near impossible. Especially, after she had her child transferred into KJ's class. All those things happened, and I brought them to you, on just about every occasion, I told you something you either blew it off or lectured me about staying away from her. Now, she has brought her craziness to your job and now you wanna take her serious. I don't know what to say to you."

I could say I told you so right now and laugh, but I'm sure that wouldn't go over well right now.

"How did the situation end?"

"She didn't leave until I threatened to call security and have her escorted out of the building."

I noticed you didn't ask her why she put that stuff in that first letter about you seeing some white woman. Seems to me like that should've been the first thing you challenged her on. I know that would've been the first thing I would've asked about if she'd lied on me. The only way I wouldn't have brought it up was if it was the truth.

"How much longer are you going to be there?"

"Caren has spoiled the fun. Looks like everybody is about ready to leave—I know that I am. I should be home before ten. Just promise me one thing."

"What?"

"If for some reason that crazy chic comes to the house, you're going to call the police rather than get into a fight with her."

"That depends on a few things."

"Like what?"

"How hard she knocks on my door, how much wine I've had, and how long it takes for the police to get here."

"Lord have mercy," Kevin said and hung up.

Chapter Fourteen

We were scheduled to fly into town the day of Marsha's holiday party. I decided to use that last day before we left to do some last-minute Christmas shopping for the kids. I was also determined to find a gift for our neighbors, Pete and Lue. I felt like they were real friends when we needed them most. Often, people claim to be your friends when the sky is clear and there are no storms brewing, but Pete and Lue were just the opposite. When they received that letter, they could have washed their hands with us, and I can't say that I would've blamed them. People have their own problems in life. No one wants to be sucked into a neighbor's drama. But they stepped up and didn't turn their backs on us. I respected and appreciated that. So, come hell or high water, there was going to be a gift under their Christmas tree from our family.

I finished my shopping around two that evening and headed home so that I could be there before school let out. Before I could place my shopping bags down the phone started to ring.

"Hello!" I said, slightly out of breath.

"Is this KJ's mother?"

"Yes, it is. Who's calling?"

"This is Principal Betty, from the school. There has been an accident."

"What kind of accident?"

"KJ was playing on the playground and has fallen from the sliding board."

"Is he okay?"

"Well, it's hard to say. There was a lot of blood. He has damage to his mouth and chin. The ambulance has—"

"Ambulance! You had to call an ambulance?"

"Umm, yes ma'am. He is currently being transported to the hospital. They are in route as we speak."

Needless to say, I was beside myself after receiving that call. So much so, that I didn't let the principal finish speaking before I ended the call. I dashed out of my house, leaving a trail of shopping bags on the floor behind me, and raced to the hospital. I was moving so fast that I beat the ambulance to the Emergency Room.

KJ suffered a lacerated chin and split lip. Both wounds required stitches, but it could have been a lot worse. I was happy the principal called me, and I was able to be at the hospital with him. But I wasn't happy with the fact that she conveniently failed to tell me that my son didn't just fall from the slide, he was pushed by another child. That revelation created the need for a conference with the principal the next day. And since that next day was the last day, the kids would be in school before their two-week Christmas break, I had to be at the conference with the principal—catching a flight to go to a Christmas party was the furthest thing from my mind.

The meeting with the principal went about as well as could be expected. The principal tried to justify why there were no teachers around supervising the kids. The other child's mother was there swearing that her boy was an angel and would never have pushed KJ unless he was provoked. And I was able to unleash a verbal assault on everyone in attendance. In the end, nothing was really accomplished other than me letting off steam.

Fortunately, the two-week holiday break allowed KJ's wounds to heal well before school started back in the New Year. He was able to start the second semester on time without missing any days.

On Christmas eve, I received a call from, Marsha, my former roommate from the University who hosted the party we were supposed to attend.

"Girl, where were you? I waited all night for you to come through the door."

"I'm so sorry, I didn't come or that I didn't get a chance to call you. KJ had an accident at school. He fell off an eight feet tall sliding board."

"What? Oh my...is he okay?"

"He'll survive. A few stitches. I think I was more shook up than him. I had to go meet with the principal and talk to the other child's parent."

"Well, I hope you gave them a piece of your mind. I can't stand those damn sliding boards. As far as I'm concerned, they should be banned from playgrounds. Them and those metal monkey bars. I don't know what numb nut came up with the idea for those things anyway. Probably someone who never had kids. Because any parent knows that when you put kids on top of stuff like that—eight feet high—that's an accident waiting to happen."

"Who you tellin'. I was just happy he only got a few scrapes that needed to be stitched. He could've broken his arm."

"Or his neck."

"Girl, I don't even wanna think about it. Let's change the subject. How was the party?"

"It was good. Would've been better if you had come."

"Well, I just told you why I couldn't make it. Kevin and I were looking forward to it. But that meeting with the principal was at the same time as our flight was to leave. I started to send Kevin there without me, but he wasn't having it."

"Girl, you never send your man to a damn party alone. These women on the prowl more than the men. Kevin is a handsome man. He would've had to beat them off with a stick the moment they figured out he was alone."

I wanted to tell her that I wasn't concerned about competing with other women for Kevin's affection because all the signs were pointing to the fact that I was already dealing with that problem where we lived.

"Tell me who showed up that was a surprise," I said trying to shift the conversation away from my husband.

Marsha didn't reply right away. Her hesitancy was long enough for me to ask the question again.

"Marsha, did you hear me? Who came that was a surprise?"

"I heard you the first time."

"Well…"

"Don't get mad, but Caren came. She spent the whole night looking for you and asking people if they knew whether you were coming."

I could feel myself getting annoyed. Marsha knew that revelation would annoy me too, which is why she was hesitant to say it.

"Wait, why was Caren there?"

"Because I invited her."

"Wait, wait, wait...I told you about the hurtful letters that woman sent how she tried to ruin my family. You agreed with me that what she did was foul. Yet, after hearing all of that you turned around and still invited her to your party. Why would you do something like that?"

"Beauty, I understand y'all have a beef, but she is my friend too," Marsha said defensively. "Besides, she promised me that she wouldn't start any mess. I made it clear to her that I wanted my event to be classy and that she needed to leave all ghetto behavior outside the party."

"But I confided in you and told you that our issues were serious enough that things could turn violent very quickly because my children were involved. I told you to not invite us if you were going to inviting them. I assumed that when you sent us an invite that they were not going to be there."

"Honestly, I thought you might've been exaggerating a little. And then when I talked to Caren, she said—"

"When you talked to Caren! So, after I told you all that stuff you went and called Caren?"

"Well Beauty, she deserved a chance to tell her side of the story. That's only right. If the situation was reversed and she had come to me first about you, I would've given you a chance to tell your side before I just uninvited you."

I could feel steam pouring out of my ears. I clinched my fist so hard that I could feel my skin stretching. If I could have reached through the phone and snatched Marsha up by the collar, I would have definitely done it.

"So, what you're saying is, you thought I was lying when I told you all that stuff about the poison pen letters and the nasty things, she said in them?"

"I never said that Beauty, all I'm saying is that I wanted to hear both sides."

"No, what you wanted to do was be messy. Honestly, I believe there is a part of you that wanted us to have an incident at the event."

"That's nonsense."

"Is it really, Marsha. Let's keep it real, it ain't like a lot happens at those parties. If we got into a big fight that would be one way to ensure that your friends would be talking about what happened for years to come."

I ended the call at that moment. I didn't need to hear anything else from my so-called friend. With friends like Marsha, you don't need enemies. So, I made my mind up that day to write Marsha, and her click of friends, off my interpersonal social associates. They were no longer friends of mine. From that day forward, they would always be classified as acquaintances.

Chapter Fifteen

Winter blew through leaving its trail of laughter and good joy. A snowstorm slapped the Midwest like we owed it money which kept everything on lock down for an entire week. By the time February came rolling around, we were all just eager to see a day with clear skies and a breeze that didn't freeze our nose hairs and make our teeth chatter.

After doing a good job getting the department's budget under control and reducing overtime, Kevin received another promotion. His second within a calendar year. This bumped his salary up by another ten thousand dollars. This gave us the means to relocate to a different county. As you might guess, I was ecstatic. This took a lot of pressure off me, because we would be out of the same neighborhood as Caren.

My husband's company assisted us in finding a new home. I thought their assistance would speed up the process, but it introduced so much bureaucracy into the relocation that what should have taken a couple of weeks ended up taking several months. To make matters more frustrating, the poison pen letters continued to come. With each letter, I started to notice a pattern.

Around the fifteenth of every month, I would receive a new letter. I continued to monitor the letters for threats. She even had the nerve in one of the letters to suggest that my husband and I, as well as our neighbors, all put our heads together and brainstorm to see if we could figure out who could be sending the letters to me. It was apparent that she was enjoying this. It was all one big game that she was getting some type of perverse pleasure out of. She wanted to sit with me and relish in the anguish I was suffering because of her crazy demented mind.

The letters continued to be typed and from different typewriters. Some contained poems and rhymes:

Oh Beauty, please don't be blue. I am not the one torturing you. Dear Beauty, can't you see it is not me, who is tormenting thee.

The craziness continued well into the spring. One night I was watching an episode of the tv show Forensic Files. The episode was about a serial arsonist. I don't remember much of the details about the show, but I do remember one line that a detective on the show said. He said: *No matter how long they get away with it, at some point, they get cocky and make a mistake.*

I'm not sure why that sentence stuck with me, but it did. In hindsight, I suspect it stuck with me because that was my prevailing sentiment whenever I received a poison pen letter from Caren. Because no one seemed to believe me or cared enough to help me, I stopped telling family and friends about the letters. They'd become desensitized to hearing about them and I'd become numb to their responses. It hurt to be ignored by people who I always thought I could trust. So, my defense mechanism became to keep my struggles to myself. I didn't tell anyone— not even Kevin on some occasions. He never knew how many letters were sent, and honestly, I don't think he cared.

Finally, in late spring it happened. After a year of dealing with Caren's crap, the beginning of the end appeared. The comment that the detective made on Forensic Files became my reality.

While standing in my window one day watching the mailman stare at the butt of a woman walking past in spandex, I saw him reach into his bag and pull out a bulky package. He shoved it into my mailbox and strolled away.

I retrieved the package and practically sprinted back through my front door. The package was addressed to me, and it had a return address on it from: KINDER CARE DAY CARE CENTER. I opened it up and found that although it was a medium sized package, inside it was just another taunting poison pen letter from Caren.

She's so stupid, I thought. *She's going through all this trouble and expending all this energy just to send me foolishness like this. She really is a sick puppy.*

I took the package outside to the backyard where we kept our garbage cans and I was about to toss into the can, when I noticed something—the address.

"Bingo!" I said aloud.

After months of sending threatening letters, Caren had finally shown her ugly poison pen hand. I went back inside and kicked off my slippers and grabbed my tennis shoes and a jacket. Like a sprinter with a gold medal in sight, I dashed out my front door, hopped in my car, and peeled out of the driveway.

The line at the post office moved at a glacial pace, but I couldn't have cared less. I was so hyped that I would have stood there even if they announced a tornado was coming.

"Next!"

"Umm yes, I need to speak to the Postmaster about an issue."

"Okay. Please stand over there while I go and get him, ma'am."

The rotund Postmaster moved slower than the line. He came to a side door with a window cut out that eliminated the need to open the door.

"How may I help you ma'am?" he asked in a nasally voice.

"I came here a few months ago and talked to you about poison pen letters I'd been receiving." The man scratched his stubbled chin and squinted at me. Suddenly, his face relaxed and his eyes widened. He pointed and said, "I do remember you."

I smiled and shoved the package into his chest.

"What do we have here?" he asked.

"I have another harassing letter sent to me via the mail. When I brought the previous letters to you, you told me there wasn't anything the postal service could do because there was no return address." I stabbed at the left corner of the package with my index finger. "That looks like a return address to me."

The chubby postmaster flashed a stained tooth smile at me and said, "It sure does. Now we're in business."

After I finished filing a formal complaint with the US Postal Service, I quickly headed over to the City attorney's office. When I walked through the door, I immediately spotted Michael Greenwell.

"You remember me?" I asked.

He took a moment to think and then pointed at me. "Poison pen letters, right?"

I smiled and nodded. "Yep."

"If you're back here that must mean you have some other kind of proof."

I held up the package. "Let's see who you believe now."

The letter was approximately eight handwritten pages long. It had the time started in the upper right-hand corner, and the time of completion on the bottom of the final page. It went on and on about her wonderful honorable charter, and how she valued our friendship to the extent that she would never do anything to cause our friendship to end. She thought very highly of me and wished me nothing but a great life. She rambled on about how our lives were so similar and fantastic. She has two children and I do too. We both work for the same company. We both have new cars and homes in the same neighborhood. We both graduated from the same University. We majored in the same field of study. We were both married to wonderful hard-working men. We had many of the same friends from school. We go to the same salon and have the same nail technician. Our children are in the same classroom. Blah blah blah for eight pages. It was like she was writing a deposition of our similar lives.

It only took Mr. Greenwell five minutes to conclude that I had enough proof for them to pursue Caren. They issued her a summons for court, The City verses Caren Ring. We were all glad to have our court date. By her placing a false return address, using a childcare, knowing I had small children she was forcing me to read a harassment letter under bogus circumstance.

As I walked out of that building, I could feel my face stretch from the wide grin that formed. I walked past a man carrying a suitcase and heading toward the entrance of the building while I was walking away from it.

"How are you doing on this fine day, ma'am?" he asked.

I flashed my wide smile in his direction and said, "No matter how long they get away with it, at some point, they get cocky and make a mistake."

The man stopped and nodded and said, "I've been a prosecuting attorney for ten years and you know what…you're right. Eventually, they all screw up and make a mistake."

Chapter Sixteen

I was blindsided by this crazy woman. She was playing a sick copycat game of me. All her weird ways were driving her to observe my life and copy from it. When I ran into her in the store years back. I had never had an interpersonal relationship with the mentally ill person. This chick had a full-blown personality and character disorder. Now, I know how it is, and let me tell you, there is nothing funny about it. In fact, it can be downright scary.

The court date was set for mid-June. It should come as no surprise that the poison pen letters also stopped coming to my house. Coincidence—I think not, the gig was up. Unfortunately, before the court date could appear, Lue would get a firsthand account of Caren.

One afternoon, I was in the mood for something sweet. I figured the kids would enjoy a little sanctioned sweetness, so I decided to make some brownies. I was in the process of stirring the batter when the phone rang.

"Hello," I said and jammed the phone in the crook of my neck.

"Beauty, this is Lue. Can you talk?"

"Yeah, I'm just sitting here cooking brownies. What's up? You sound a little winded."

"I finally met her."

"Who?"

"Crazy Caren."

I nearly dropped the mixer bowl. I stopped mixing and leaned against the counter.

"What happened?"

"I ran into her at the school where I work."

"But how would she know where you work?"

"I know, you and I know and apparently, Caren knew that too. She took a substitute teaching job at the school. Anyway, I was collecting some items from my locker, and suddenly, I heard someone call my full name. I turned around and she walked up to me and asked, 'Are you Lue Smith?' I spoke as friendly as I normally speak to someone, I acknowledged her. And then she said, 'We've never met in person, but I'm Caren, and I just want to tell you that I am not the person writing those letters.'"

"No, she didn't."

"Yes, she did," Lue replied.

"What happened next?"

"Girl, I was so creeped out by the confrontation, that I didn't know what to do. I don't know how to handle a crazy woman. So, I slowly began to walk down the hall to the parking lot. Caren followed me the entire way. All she seemed concerned with was trying to convince me that she was not the person involved in the poison pen letters I received."

"Were there any other coworkers around?"

"Nobody. Any other time the campus is crawling with people, but on today of all days, it was a ghost town. Girl. I was so frightened and creeped out by the fact that this woman knew me by sight! I wouldn't have been able to pick her out in a police lineup, but she knows my name, my home address, where I worked and even when I get off."

"I told you she's a stalker."

"Yes, you warned me. I can't deny that."

"So, what happened after she followed you out the building?"

"I was walking slow on purpose. For one, I didn't want her to see which car I was going to get into. Secondly, I was kind of hoping that the slow pace would give her time to say whatever she felt she needed to say and then leave. But wouldn't you know it…that didn't work."

"And there was no one in the parking lot who could help you?"

"Girl, I'm telling you, I've never seen anything so crazy. That entire parking lot was empty. My car, and maybe three or four others, were the only cars left in the lot. So, we're just standing in the middle of the lot. Caren is still rambling on about her innocence. When I tried to end the conversation, she just stood there looking crazy. That's when it dawned on me."

"What?"

"I recognized the remaining cars in the parking lot and knew who they belonged to. I asked where she was parked, and she didn't answer. Then I asked her if she needed a ride and before I could get the question out of my mouth, she jumped into the front seat of my car."

"You gave her a ride?"

"I didn't have much of a choice. She opened the door so quickly and hopped in. I was so freaked out. I even thought about walking away from my own car and leaving her sitting in it. I mean, I didn't know if she had a weapon on her or if she planned to hurt me…I just didn't know."

"Where did you drop her off?"

"That was probably the best part of the whole story. She asked me to let out around the corner. I dropped her off in front of a house and pulled off. Girl, when I got home, I immediately called Pete."

"What did he say?"

"He blew a gasket. He wanted to grab his gun and go look for her. I managed to talk him off the ledge. After we hung up, that's when I decided to call you to let you know about this craziness."

"Child, I've been knowing she was crazy. Everybody else is just starting to see what I've been trying to say all along."

"Well, I witnessed it firsthand today and I can't wait until that hearing so I can tell the judge what she did to me."

"Trust me, we're all ready to go the court and get this nut job away from our lives."

We were all present for the court date: Lue and her husband, me and Kevin, and the attorney. Caren entered with her husband, Robert, and her mother. As luck would have it, our attorney was a substitute who had no paperwork about the case. Fortunately, I had my briefcase with all my documentation: police reports, complaints to the post office, filings to the city attorney office, all her letters, cards, poems, packages—I was ready even if the person representing me wasn't.

When my attorney shared with the judge all the evidence, as well as the letters from the neighbors. How she went to my husband employment, as well as her going to my neighbor's job and corralling her up after her day had ended, following her into the parking lot. I also stated we attend professional, community, and social events in common. and that I should not be made to feel uncomfortable in those settings, because I am the victim.

The judged ruled that she was not to come within 500 feet of me or my family members, and because of the multiple varied orchestrated encounters and incidents the case would remain open not closed; in the possibility that she might act out at some future date.

I was so relieved to get rid of the miserable stain in my life. Caren was gone. All had been exposed and the courts had delt with her and it was on paper.

Six months later, we moved to a northern county, and I started working in a different district. Life was good—until Christmas when I received another mailing with no return address. A poison chain letter and a Christmas card. It was Caren's way of letting me know that she knew where I was, she was still obsessed and willing to risk restrictive actions to keep her focus on me.

I attended my twenty-year Christmas reunion celebration at my university. It was a huge event. While sitting at my assigned table I looked up and standing in front of me was none other than crazy

Caren. She glared at me like an angry dog with rabies.

I was not going to let her try to intimidate me, so I stood up and crossed my arms and staired back at her. Her husband appeared at our table and lead her away. That was the last University event that I ever attended.

Fifteen years later, and I would have gladly told anyone who asked that Caren was a distant memory. But crazy has no expiration date. I was reminded of this fact after I was involved in a hit and run car wreck and sustained several serious injuries. I became a patient of a neurologist/internist in a different county. I had been a patient there for a few years.

The way the clinic was set up, you would be seen by the doctor and then you would receive testing and physical therapy in another part of the building. When I finished my physical therapy session one day, I observed crazy Caren entering the doctor's office. I recalled how she set up the run in at the parent teacher conference from years ago. So, I informed the entire staff that I would no longer sign in and out on the public paperwork. I explained that I had been in litigation with one of their patients who had been able to follow me by viewing my appointment schedule in the pass. They asked for the person's name, but I did not give it to them. I explained it would not be necessary. I would be in control of my visits.

Well, at my next visit, they told me her name…Caren Ring. They said, she came in and asked for all my information. She told them we were old friends from college, and I would be thrilled if she could contact me. We could catch up on our lives. Fortunately for me, they told her it was against the law to give out patient information. Caren insisted that I would not mind, but they did not give it to her.

After I learned that Caren was still trying to track me down, I never made an appointment in writing. Nor did I ever list the day of the week or time that I would be in to see my doctor—that didn't matter.

A few months later, after one of my physical therapy sessions, I was exiting the clinic and I heard an unfamiliar voice call out my full name. I instantly recognized this behavior from years ago with my neighbor Lue. Her account of when she was disrupted with Caren's stalking at her work. I just continued to walk out. The woman followed me to the door. When she caught up to me, she continued to engage me in conversation.

"Beauty, don't you remember me?"

"No, I don't."

"Well, I remember you. You once came to a Bar B Q at my home in Flint."

As I continued to walk, she continued to follow.

"I got married and moved to Florida, but my marriage didn't last."

I was walking down the long handicap ramp by this time. My car was parked in the first handicap parking space by the door. As she realized I was not going to fall for the trap they had concocted to hold me up for her crazy friend to appear and harass me, the mystery woman yelled, "I heard your husband left you for a white woman!"

I was about to climb inside my car but paused long enough to look back at her and say, "Shit happens."

Ten years have passed since that last confrontation with Caren's friend. I haven't seen or heard from Caren, in any way or form, since. But I must give Caren some credit...if it hadn't been for her, I wouldn't have known about the affair Kevin was having. And yes...after our divorce he married his white woman coworker.

Chapter Seventeen

ell, that's my story. As disturbing and crazy as it may sound, that's the truth, the whole truth, and nothing but the truth. So, tell me Gary…have I scared you off with my truth?"

"I'm still sitting here, aren't I?"

"Yes, you are."

"Well, that proves that I'm not scared by your back story. I must admit, it was crazy. I mean, I've heard stories about men stalking women. I've even heard stories about women stalking men. But I've never in my life heard a story about a woman stalking another woman; especially when there wasn't some type of romantic connection. Now, I must ask you this and please don't get mad."

"Let me give you an answer right now because I know what you're about to ask me. No…Caren and I were never in any way romantically connected. For some reason, the woman just gravitated to me and seemed to want my life—or at least wanted to be a part of my life. At every turn, she tried to inject herself into my world. It started when we first met in college and never stopped."

"Excuse me folks, are you ready for dessert?"

"Umm, yes. I'll have a slice of your cheesecake."

"Alright, that's one slice of our famous New York style cheesecake for the lovely lady. Sir, would you like some dessert?"

"Yeah, I think I'll have the same thing my lovely date is having. A slice of cheesecake and a cup of coffee."

"Ma'am, would you like coffee too? We have an amazing pecan flavored chicory."

"That sounds great. I'll try that."

"Great. Give me a few minutes and I'll be back with your orders."

I can't believe I just spilled my guts to this man. He says he's not scared off by that story, but I'm not so sure about that. I don't expect him to just get up and leave me in this restaurant, but I'll be surprised if he returns my phone calls after tonight. Honestly, if he told me a story like that I don't know if I'd return his phone calls afterwards. Life is hard enough, who wants to have to deal with a person with a crazy past?

"What's wrong, Beauty?"

"Nothing."

"Umm hmm. Now, you know I don't believe you. I know you aren't turned off by this atmosphere. I mean look around...the jazz band is outstanding, our diner was great, the ambiance is amazing, and this has been one of the best conversations I've ever had on a date."

"Well, if you decided that you didn't want to be bothered with me now, I'd understand."

"Stop being silly and give me your hand."

"Why, are you going to propose?"

"No, I'm not going to propose, but I want you to feel me when I say this. I am extremely attracted to you, and I want to get to know you better. Whatever you went through in your past doesn't change that fact. I mean, you already said that the situation with the crazy lady is a thing of your past. It's not like she's still stalking you. Now, do you feel the same about me? Do you want to give *us* a shot?"

I can't believe this. He's really into me despite what I've told him. I never thought I'd get a second shot at love. But I'm really starting to feel like Gary could be the one. This could be my chance to start a new life with the perfect man. And he's right...crazy lady is a chapter in my life that I've moved on from. It's time for me to stop fighting this and go with it.

"Gary, I really like you too. And yes, I do want to give us a…"

What the hell. Wait, wait, wait, I must be seeing things. No…I'm not. My vision is perfectly fine. I'll be damned…Caren is sitting at that table over there. And the heifer is smiling at me.

"Beauty, are you okay? You look like you just saw a ghost."

"Umm, I…I think I just did."

"Excuse me."

"Umm, Gary, I think we should leave."

"Is everything okay?"

"I thought everything was okay, but now, I'm not so sure."

THE END